COMMUTER WIDOW

COMMUTER WIDOW

LOUIS LORRAINE

CUTTING EDGE

ISBN-13: 978-1-954840-14-0

Published by
Cutting Edge Books
PO Box 8212
Calabasas, CA 91372
www.cuttingedgebooks.com

PART 1

CHAPTER ONE

A S soon as the children were settled in front of the television screen, Susan Wladek laid down the dish towel and seated herself across from her husband at the dining room table. Paul had already spread his papers across the table, had put on his black horn-rimmed glasses and was scowling over his figures, referring often to the set of account books at his elbow.

"Paul."

"Um."

"I have to talk to you. Things have gotten so bad, we have to do something."

"Um."

He was not listening. Paul Wladek hardly ever listened to her when she tried to talk seriously to him. Susan clasped her shaking hands tightly together. All their married life, Paul had been the one who decided matters—chose the car, bought the furniture, worked out the budget, yelled at the repairmen. He was a forceful man, with a European's ideas of how a home should be run. Born in Poland, he had fought with the American Army in World War II. Afterward, he had come to this country, become a citizen, and built up a flourishing one-man importing business. She had rarely questioned his judgment. But when he had suddenly decided, without even telling her, to buy a house in a community thirty miles from Franklin, she had finally found the willpower to protest.

It had done her no good. As soon as school was over in June, they had moved out of their comfortable apartment into a new, badly constructed split-level on a muddy, weed-covered acre of land.

"The children have been in school two weeks. They're bored and restless. They had this material a year ago in the Franklin schools. I want to move back to town. It isn't too late to start them in school again. They can catch up. And they miss their friends so much!"

Paul frowned, and she knew he was finally paying attention. She went on swiftly.

"I miss my friends, too. There just isn't anyone here who cares about music and art and—"

"Bridge?" snapped Paul sarcastically, without looking up from his papers. "I'll bet you miss your bridge club!"

"Yes, I do. Very much." How much, she could not make him understand. The girls in the club had been friends most of their lives. It was not really the bridge that Susan missed. It was being able to talk to the girls every week, to relax and gossip and laugh, and forget her problems for a while. She had hoped to go into town at least once a month. But so far she had not got in at all, except once to take Pamela to the dentist in an emergency. The bus trip had been a nightmare, an hour and a half each way—the bus jolting, crowded, filled with exhaust fumes. Susan clenched her hands and went on.

"You don't mind this, I know. You aren't here enough to know how lonely it is, with no one to talk to, no one—"

"There is the boy next door. He helps you, as you often tell me."

Duane's only a boy, only eighteen. And he has helped. I couldn't have managed without him. This house is too much for me, Paul. I'm exhausted. And the yard is impossible. It's too bumpy to mow easily—"

"I said I would do it, but you never waited for me to find the time."

She bit her lip. Paul was so unfair! The summer had been unbearably hot; Paul had stayed in town often over the weekends in a friend's air-conditioned apartment. If she had waited for him to do the yard, the weeds would have grown too high for the mower.

"The point is, Paul, this house isn't right for us! The children and I won't be happy till we move back to town. Paul, there isn't even a library here! And the church is five miles away. We aren't able to go when you stay in town over the weekend."

"I will be here more often this winter. The work is letting up a little."

Her patience was exhausting itself against his stolid indifference. "Oh, why did you have to buy a house in this horrible place?" She cried, "Why didn't you ask me first? What made you do such a crazy thing?"

Now at last he looked up, his dark eyes cold with displeasure. "This was a bargain. I bought fast because if I had waited I would have lost the opportunity. You knew I was looking for a house."

"In town, yes—not out here, miles from civilization!"

"You are exaggerating again, Susan. There is an excellent shopping center only a mile away. And we are right on the edge of a town with a population of five thousand."

Susan swallowed hard. What argument would reach him, what persuasion? Her husband was always so firmly convinced he was right...

The children came unexpectedly to her aid. She had not realized they were listening, but now Pam switched off the TV. She and Harvey came into the dining room.

Harvey, calm, dark-eyed and logical for his nine years, began shrewdly enough. "You had a pretty good idea, Dad, buying this house. Why pay rent to somebody else?"

Paul relaxed and looked at his son fondly. "I'm glad that you agree with me. Your mother seems to think I am always wrong."

Pam exchanged a quick, secret look with her mother. Her black, straight hair set off her vivid blue eyes. Everyone said she was the image of her mother, but Susan thought Pam was much prettier than she had ever been. Pam had a confidence and mature wisdom that Susan felt she lacked at 33.

"Gee, I don't think you're wrong, Dad. It's just that I think it'd be smart to go back to Franklin before Pam and me lose out on our school work. You see, Dad, they aren't really up on anything out here. The classes are too crowded. There's fifty-eight in my class and sixty-four in Pam's. And we go awfully slow. We had lots of this stuff last year in Franklin. And Pam says she had some of her stuff two years ago."

Paul's mouth twisted sarcastically. "Well, I'm sure if you children are patient, the rest of the class will catch up to you. Just remember, you are not grown up yet. Your place is to listen and do what you are told—not tell your father and mother what to do!"

"That isn't the point, Paul! Harvey was coming along so well in his art class, and Pam in her music—"

"Enough!" Paul slammed his fist on the table and shoved back his chair. "Do I send my children to school to play or to work? We are here. This is our home. You will go to school with the other children, and learn what they learn."

"But, Dad—" Pam began.

"I don't want hear another word! Be careful, young lady. You are not too old yet to be spanked."

Pam went white, staring at her father. She adored him, and could not bear to have him speak harshly to her.

Susan intervened hurriedly. "Go back to the television, children," she said. "It's time for the mystery show you like."

She picked up the dish towel and went to the kitchen. From the kitchen window, she could see the Ackerman's house next door. Mrs. Ackerman and Duane lived in a big, run-down farmhouse that looked out of place now, surrounded by raw one-acre tracts and identical split-level houses.

Beyond were muddy fields, a desolate countryside bare of trees, a crumbling red barn. She had tried many times that summer, on walks with the children, to find a beauty spot worthy of her camera, but there was none. The bulldozers had worked too much havoc. She had taken few photographs, and her small income from prizes and published camera studies would be even smaller this year.

Paul worked at the dining room table until eleven, when he gathered up his papers and went to bed with only a gruff "Good night" flung in her direction. Soon after, Susan went to the guest bedroom which had been hers since the first few nights in this house. She and Paul had quarreled with such frightening violence in their first days here, that she had started sleeping in the guest room, and had gradually moved all her things into it.

They had never quarreled seriously before. During the hot summer months, Susan had grown to realize that this was not because they had had nothing to disagree about. It was because she had never stood up to her husband until now.

This weekend, she resolved, she must keep after Paul again and again, even if he should erupt in violent fury.

The next day was Friday. Susan remembered, glancing at the calendar, that the next evening was the first concert of her favorite series, the Franklin Symphony Concert series.

She mentioned it to Paul. "You did get the tickets, didn't you?" she asked, as she poured his second second cup of coffee.

"No, I didn't get them."

"You didn't forget! Oh, Paul!" She was startled, almost horrified. They had gone to the concerts every year since their marriage, and before that she had gone with school friends ever since high school.

Paul looked resentful. "No, I did not forget. I thought it was not worthwhile to get season tickets, since we probably will not make it very often."

"Oh, Paul!"

The children were watching anxiously, not eating. She forgot her own rule about not arguing in front of the children. "You know that's my favorite concert series. I've gone for years!"

"You ought to be tired of it then," he muttered.

"We could go in tomorrow and see if we can get some seats. I'm not going to give up music, too!"

"You have the record player. And besides, I am staying in town this weekend. I have much work to do."

Susan could find no words to protest as he produced a suitcase, got his hat and huge briefcase and said, "Goodbye. I will see you Monday night."

"But, Paul," she said at last, running after him. "The concert! What about the concert?"

It was a small point, after all the bitter disappointments of the summer, but it seemed to her the most unbearable hurt of them all. He knew how she loved music—how eagerly she anticipated the programs!

Paul looked sorry, but unwilling to admit it. "Well, get a baby sitter then, and take the bus in. Telephone me at Jack's. Maybe I can meet you for the concert." He kissed her cheek briefly, then got in the car and drove off.

Harvey rushed out of the house. "Is he gone? Gee, I thought he'd drive us to school."

Now Susan noticed it was beginning to rain—a light misty rain. The clouds above were dark grey and beyond were ominous black clouds. It was going to pour. How selfish Paul could be! The children had to walk a mile and a half to school, either on the highway, dangerously clogged with cars, or in the mud beside the highway.

She went back into the house and helped the children find boots, raincoats, umbrellas. She would have liked to keep them home, but both children were proud of their perfect attendance records. She watched them go with the helpless feeling of a shepherd watching small lambs dangerously close to a precipice.

She must think of some way, however drastic, to help them and herself.

She went back to the kitchen to do the dishes. Then she made the beds and dusted, always mechanically, her mind going around in a squirrel cage of doubts and confusions. Was Paul right? Would everything work out for the best, after all?

She turned on the record player, and put on her favorite Chopin records. The brilliant, lovely piano music filled the house with melody, and she was soothed. But it reminded her also that the concert tomorrow night would go on without her. The house lights would dim, the orchestra cease its dissonant tuning, a hush would come in the warm perfumed dimness, then the conductor would walk out. And the music would begin. The music would begin, and go on and on, but Susan would not hear it.

CHAPTER TWO

THE light, misty rain continued for an hour and a half. Susan was grateful that it did not become a downpour until the children were safely at school. They ate in the school cafeteria at noon, and by mid-afternoon it might let up so they would not get soaked coming home.

About nine-thirty, the light tapping of the rain against the windows changed to a heavier tattoo, and the rain blew in gusts of grey torrents which blotted out the highway. Susan, peering out the window, noticed a black object at the far end of the side lawn. It was the power mower. She had gotten it out yesterday afternoon, but the stubborn clumps of grass and weeds had kept jamming the blades. The mower would get rusty unless she brought it in. She hesitated, but finally flung on her raincoat and dashed out the side door to rescue the machine.

It was stuck just where she had left it in disgust. She pulled and tugged at it, the rain half-blinding her. Her legs and feet were soaked when she heard young Duane Ackerman's voice beside her.

"Go on back to the house! I'll get it—go on!"

Duane was dressed in boots and raincoat, and looked far more competent to deal with the weather and the mower than Susan felt. She yelled back, "Thanks!" and ran to the house as a fresh deluge swept across the open yard.

She watched from the kitchen window as he struggled with the mower, finally lifting it and half carrying, half dragging it into the garage. Paul had bought it second hand, another of his "bargains."

Susan flung open the breezeway door, called to Duane, "Come on in—I'll fix you some breakfast!"

He came in, huge and dripping, and shivered near the register until he was warm again. She took his raincoat and spread it over a chair to drip on the kitchen floor. Then she started fixing the hot chocolate he liked so well.

He sat down at the kitchen table, watched her movements with the intent interest of a child. His mother worked in Franklin, leaving early in the morning and not returning home until six in the evening. Duane himself worked at the shopping center in New Harmony from 1 to 10 P.M., so he saw his mother only on Sundays.

"There. Drink that—it'll warm you up."

He drank the chocolate, ate four pieces of toast and jam. Susan went on cleaning up in the kitchen and dining room.

When his hunger seemed appeased, she asked, "Did you have to work hard yesterday?"

He nodded. "Had a mess of people in. Understand some more folks moved into the new flat east of town."

"You must be tired. You don't get enough sleep."

He shrugged. "Hard to sleep after it gets daylight. Let me do that." He took the sweeper from her and emptied the dirt from it efficiently. Duane was good around the house. Susan suspected he did most of the housework at home.

"Thanks, Duane." She remembered Paul's callous indifference to her hard work, to her pleadings to go back to the city. This boy, untrained and immature, was more considerate of her, more helpful than her own husband. "You're too good to me—I'll get spoiled."

Duane smiled, pleased. His short, blonde hair curled in small ringlets all over his head. Susan felt like touching his hair, and was annoyed with herself.

"Aw, no," he said. "I would like to help."

Susan sat down on a kitchen chair, lit a cigarette. Not for the first time she noticed how strongly and cleanly Duane was built, how gracefully he moved. Did he think of her as a woman? Was it possible for her to be attractive, desirable, to a boy like this?

Blushing, she put the thought out of her mind. She did not know what had gotten into her. Probably it was the exhausting quarrel with Paul, the grey day—all the frustrations of the past weeks coming to a head. The best thing to do was to keep busy and forget it.

She stubbed out her cigarette, gathered up Duane's breakfast dishes and took them to the sink. She ran the hot water, closed the drain. "Hand me the soap powder, will you, Duane?"

"Where is it, here?" He came over to the counter, opened the cabinets underneath.

"No, on top," she said. Misunderstanding, he began looking on the counter top, behind a collection of detergents and bleaches.

"No, not there," said Susan. "Never mind—let me." Without stopping to dry her hands, she leaned past him, opening the cabinet door over his head. She had to put her weight on one hand, rise on tiptoe to get past his big body. She realized abruptly that she was much closer than she had meant to be; but in a moment she would have the box she wanted—

Then her wet hand slipped on the counter top, throwing her weight against him. Off balance, she clutched at him for support.

It lasted for only a moment, but for that moment her body was pressed tight against his, her breasts flattened against his broad back, her thighs touching his legs. She straightened, flushed and embarrassed, tingling from the brief contact. "I'm sorry!" she said.

Duane had turned. He was flushed, too, his eyes brilliant as he stared at her. "Don't be—sorry," he said with difficulty. As if by instinct, his hands went to her waist. She could feel the muscular hardness of his palms through her dress.

"Could I kiss you?" he asked humbly. "Just once?"

"Oh, Duane..." She hesitated, not wanting to hurt him.

"I guess I shouldn't have asked," he said.

"Well, just once," she said faintly. Surprised at herself, she stood close to him, cupped his earnest face in her hands, and pressed her mouth to his. The touch of his lips gave her a sudden hot thrill she had not expected. She had only wanted to kiss a lonely boy... but this was a man's demanding mouth on hers.

She broke away quickly. His arms still held her, his mouth seeking hers. "Susan? Please?"

She pushed his arms away, gently but firmly. "Duane, you're awfully sweet. But you know this isn't right—we mustn't."

"I know," he said in a low voice.

"Now don't you be sorry," she said cheerfully. "It was something that happened, and it's over, and we must forget about it.'

"You mean you're not angry with me?"

"Of course I'm not!"

Duane hesitated a moment, then crossed the room and gathered up his raincoat and hat. "I better go now," he said, "but—" With a swift motion he came back to her, raised one of her hands and kissed it gently. Then he was gone.

Pamela and Harvey were restless on Saturdays. Their weekend homework was "old stuff."

Susan persuaded them to work out the "stupid silly problems" and write the "icky essays." Then, as a reward, she got out some books and read to them about more advanced matters, science and geography for Harvey, and art and music for Pamela, illustrating the music material with records. Both the children seemed keenly interested and stimulated.

"Oh, Mom, this is so much better than that stupid school!" said Pamela. "Why couldn't we stay home and you teach us?"

Susan smoothed back Pam's black, silky hair. Her pretty baby girl was growing up so fast—her thin legs carrying her daily into unknown situations, where Susan could not protect her. She stifled an anxious sigh.

"I don't know enough for that, Pam," she said, then added cheerily, "But we'll try to work things out. Let me have a little more time."

"Are you going to talk Dad into moving back to the city?" asked Harvey.

"Is that what you children really want? Don't you think in time that you'll like the kids here, and get used to things?"

Harvey and Pam exchanged a quick look. Pam said, "I guess we will—if you want us to, Mom."

But there was something held back, something reserved and strange underneath her obedience, something almost frightened.

On Sunday afternoon she went for a long walk with Pam and Harvey. She took with her a favorite camera that had taken many good black and whites. Some had won prizes. Her city scenes had been highly praised by a state magazine, *Field and City Street,* that had bought many of her photos. She was determined to find something to photograph, even in the bleak landscape around New Harmony.

The October day was brilliant with golden sunshine. The sky was a clear, vivid blue with only a few translucent threads of white clouds trailing across the horizon. A sky-writing airplane drew a slow line of white smoke behind it.

At least there was the sky, thought Susan. She could always look up to the sky. But then, when she looked down again to the muddy fields, the row of ugly new houses, many unoccupied, some not even finished, she felt a terrible depression of spirit. Why did men make such desolation?

"It's ugly, isn't it, Mom?" Pam said, with a shiver. Her red tam was a spot of color against the bleakness. "I wonder why the bulldozers knocked down all the trees and left that mess over there?

Why didn't they leave some trees? Now people will have to plant new ones, and it takes years to make a tree grow."

"Maybe they weren't thinking," said Harvey. "Some people don't think ahead. They just rip up things and get sorry later."

Susan tried to distract their attention. "See if you can help me find a picture," she said. "I haven't taken any all summer. See if you can find one for me to take."

"Even an ugly one, Mom?" asked Harvey.

"Yes, even an ugly one."

One reason she enjoyed being with the children was that they were so honest. Why weren't adults honest? Children had not learned yet to be tactful or silent or lying. Their honesty hurt, sometimes, but it was cleansing.

Pam said, "There's that old barn. Could that be a picture, with that muddy lane and the curving broken-down fence?"

Susan looked at the scene thoughtfully. It seemed to epitomize the neglected, run-down condition of the land around New Harmony. Always, before, she had tried to find beauty, to take pictures that would reveal the hidden beauty of a scene.

Well, if there was only ugliness here, she would photograph it—the stark grimness that she saw—and even enjoy the ugliness.

"Yes, Pam, that's a good one. Let's cross the road. I'll take it with the fence framing the scene."

Few cars were on the highway that Sunday afternoon. No one would drive out here for pleasure, she thought, as she checked the light meter and made the camera adjustments. She took several pictures of the barn from across the road, then they walked a dozen yards farther and she took several more. They re-crossed the road, walked a distance down the muddy lane, and she took more from several angles. Harvey and Pam watched her with keen interest as she worked.

"That old barn is where one of the gangs has their hangout," Harvey observed as they finally strolled on down the highway.

"Gangs! What gangs?" asked Susan.

"Oh—the kids. You know." Harvey glanced uneasily at Pamela, who was staring down at the muddy path beside the highway. "There's some high school kids and some grade school kids. They—well, they go around together. For fun, you know."

"Oh." For a moment she was relieved. She had been thinking of the black-leather-jacketed juvenile delinquents, so often in the paper. Of course they would not be like that, committing theft and murder and rape, not in this dull suburbia. "You don't mean a tough gang, like criminals."

"Aw, no!" said Harvey. "They just mess around. Having fun."

"What do they do in the barn?" asked Susan, frowning across at the sagging red building. "Why do they need a hangout?"

"Oh, they talk," said Harvey vaguely. "And they get away from their folks. At least, that's what one fellow told me. I've never gone."

"I should hope not!" said his mother sharply.

"I haven't been asked. You have to be asked," he said.

"You're too young, anyway," said Pamela. "They don't let people in till they're over twelve."

"But if you're twelve and you aren't asked in any gang—boy, you might as well not live around here," said Harvey. "They make it tough for outside kids."

Pamela frowned at him.

"Tough!" said Susan. "What do you mean?"

"He just means they tease a lot," said Pamela hastily. "Why don't we walk back toward town, Mom? There's not much to take along here. And I saw a scene on the way to school the other day. I think you'd like it, just a few blocks beyond our house. There's real pretty tree with a funny shaped tree beside it, and a goldfish pond."

Susan allowed herself to be distracted. She looked at their house critically as she passed, trying to see it as a stranger would. It looked raw and unfinished, yes, but wasn't there strength and some beauty in it? No, she thought, with a sigh. It was sprawling, awkward, badly shaped, inconvenient. And the yard was like a raw wound. It would take years to fix it up, to bring out some beauty in it.

Was it worth it, to live here? Something was wrong with this town, something the children knew and felt. For the first time in her life, Pamela was covering up the truth. She must have a long talk with Pamela alone very soon.

"There, Mom, that's the scene I meant." Pamela pointed toward a house, painted with more courage than taste in pink and golden brown. In front of the house were the two trees Pam had noticed, and a small goldfish pond.

The scene was not beautiful. The grass had large bare spots, the fish pond was cracked—the cement had been poured with unskilled hands. One of the trees was dying. It looked to Susan like a pitiful attempt to beautify ugliness, and attempt that had not succeeded. Someone who lived there cared about beauty, and had worked hard to find it; but he had failed.

"Isn't that a good picture, Mom?" asked Pam, hopefully. "See, there's even some flowers."

A few asters straggled across the front of the house.

She would take this too, Susan decided, savagely. She would take the house, with its pathetic dignity, the yard, with its pitiful landscaping.

"Yes, I think this will be good." She adjusted the camera, took shots from several angles. She caught the dying tree, the drooping flowers, the deep crack in the pond. She thought, "I'll call the series *Suburban*."

She didn't know whether *Field and City Streets* bought pictures like these. She did not recall seeing anything like them in the magazine.

The pictures made her more aware than ever of the pitiful emptiness of suburban life. They walked farther into town, and she took many more pictures—a weed-filled patch threatening to overwhelm a grassy lot next to it, a drainage ditch beside children's swings, bedraggled flowers in a muddy bed, a window box of geraniums on a house where the paint had peeled off in long, ugly strips.

"Gee, Mom," Harvey finally said, "I don't think some of these pictures are going to be pretty at all."

"Life in this town is not very pretty, Harvey," said Susan. She was tired, but she still felt a savage exhilaration. "I think the pictures will be honest. That's important too. It's good to find beauty. But honesty is good too."

"There's the bowling alley," said Harvey. They were approaching the huge shopping center where Duane worked. Susan looked at it with interest. This was the life that Duane knew. He walked back and forth to work past the ugly houses, the weed-covered lots, the muddy ditches, to—this. A hugh black-topped parking lot, store after huge store, garish with lights and bright-colored signs the plate glass windows crammed with colorful goods on display. Duane worked in the grocery.

At one end of the shopping center was a large bowling alley. Cars were parked nearby. Men and boys lounged near the entrance.

"There's Fred Goss," said Harvey. Susan turned to look.

"Don't point, Harvey," said Pamela sharply.

"Which one is he?" Susan was curious. "Is he a friend of yours, Harvey?"

"Aw, no! He's an older guy. He's sixteen."

They were walking past about twenty feet from the bowling alley. Susan saw now that most of the group consisted of young boys, about twelve to fourteen. The "older boys" were approximately sixteen or seventeen.

"Hey, Harvey!" one boy yelled.

"Don't answer!" said Pamela savagely. "Let's go back home, Mom!"

Susan was quite willing. She did not like the looks of the crowd. As they turned and walked across the parking lot toward the road, someone else yelled.

"Hey, Pam! Hey, Pam!"

Pam kept her head rigidly toward the road. Her cheeks were flushed.

"They're just teasing," said Harvey anxiously. He kept turning to look back.

"Don't look at them, silly!" snapped Pam.

"Hey, Pam! Come on back! Hey, Pam!"

Several boys were yelling at them. Susan could not hear the words distinctly. Pam walked so fast she was close to running, to get out of earshot.

They walked a long way down the road before Susan finally said, "Let's slow down. I'm out of breath."

They stopped, and Pam got out her handkerchief and mopped her eyes. "They're awful!" she burst out. "They're just awful!" Her voice cracked.

"Aw, they don't mean anything." But Harvey glanced back over his shoulder.

"I don't understand what's going on," said Susan. She felt bewildered and vaguely frightened. Nothing like this had ever happened to them in Franklin. "Do you know those children? Are they in your school?"

"Some of them are in my class," said Pam. "They all—tease me. They always tease the new ones."

"But there were older boys there," said Susan, half to herself.

"It's Fred Goss and his gang," said Harvey. "They hang around the bowling alley."

"Why?" asked Susan.

Harvey's serious face was puzzled. "I don't know, Mom. I guess it's because there's no place else to go. Except the barn."

"They're the ones who have their hangout in the barn?"

"Yes. There isn't much in New Harmony, see, except the drive-in movies. And they don't start till dark."

Susan shuddered. This dull, quiet town was full of lively children and young people, restless, full of mischief, with no safe outlets for their energy. What would happen to them? What could they do but explode into anti-social behavior? No one seemed to care. No one did anything about it.

Back home, Susan turned on the record player, and put on some of the Tchaikowsky that Pamela especially liked. The strains of the lilting "Sleeping Beauty" ballet helped lift them all out of the depression they felt.

Harvey suggested popcorn. He was always hungry. Susan popped some corn, then she read to them for a long time that evening.

The music, the words of books, the warmth of their affection for each other helped shut out the outside world. But whenever Susan raised her head from reading, she could see the darkness at the windows, a darkness that seemed to press in toward them, threatening to fill their house with its fears and hates.

CHAPTER THREE

PAUL came home Monday evening, tired, irritable and withdrawn. Susan could say nothing to him yet about her fears. She was still too angry about his deserting them. She must get over her anger, and make an effort to present the matter to him calmly and logically.

Tuesday evening she decided on impulse to drive into town with Paul the next morning. She would do some shopping, then have lunch with her Wednesday Bridge Club friends. In the back of her mind was a hope that one of them might be able to help her find a solution to the problem she faced.

On the way in, she thought about whom she would ask. Miriam Denlinger was thoughtful and intelligent; she would have good advice to offer. Nancy Alter had recently had a divorce; she was still bitter and upset; it would be better not to ask her.

Betty Lorrimer was younger and rather flighty, and thought everything her husband did was absolutely perfect and brilliant. Susan's mouth twisted. She had thought so herself about Paul—until just recently.

Jill Ohms was her closest friend. She had known Jill since grade school. They had gone to parties, concerts, plays, double dates—right through to marriage. And for years the Ohms and the Lamberts had had season tickets together for the Franklin Orchestra series. Yes, she was the one Susan would talk to. Jill would know what advice to give her.

About halfway to town, she realized she had not said a word to Paul since they had started. She glanced over at him, meaning to say something pleasant, but the look on his face startled her. He was scowling at the cars ahead; his hands were gripping the wheel tightly.

He muttered, "Those swine."

"What? Who?" asked Susan, peering at the road ahead. She had not driven since she was married, and was less conscious of driving conditions than a driver would be. She could not see anything wrong. The cars seemed to be lined up on the highway, moving forward at a good pace toward Franklin.

"They are dragging," said Paul impatiently. "Some people drive so damn slow! I want to get to town early. I've got a lot of work to do." He swore under his breath.

He watched his chance like an angry cat, then stepped on the gas and roared past several cars, slipped in ahead of them, missing one by a narrow margin, then fretted because the pace was as slow as ever.

All the way to town he drove like that, taking reckless chances to pass cars and trucks, then cursing when he had to slow down behind the next cars. By the time they reached town, he was nervous and irritable, and left Susan with scarcely a word at the department stores.

Susan watched him go with a sigh of relief. She went to get a cup of coffee, and sat for half an hour, idly watching the crowds, before she began shopping.

What was wrong with Paul? He had always been a hard worker, serious, intent on getting ahead. But lately he seemed to be driving himself as furiously and illogically as he had driven the car this morning. There was no reason for it. His importing business was doing well. His income was increasing steadily.

Something was bothering him, causing his absentmindedness, his irritation with the family, his outbursts of temper.

When her shopping was done, Susan yielded to temptation and ordered several new records. If she were going to be denied her concerts in town, she should be entitled to something by way of compensation. Then she ordered several books that she could read aloud to the children.

When she gave her new address, the clerk showed surprise.

"Oh, Mrs. Wladek, I thought you lived in town."

"No. My husband bought a house quite a distance from town."

"New Harmony! Well, that sounds like a charming place," said the clerk. "I'll send these out as soon as they arrive, Mrs. Wladek. Thank you so much."

Susan walked out slowly, enjoying the colorful lights, the displays, the well-dressed crowd, the quiet voices. This was the world she loved, the world of politeness, beauty, pleasure. What good was it to have money and leisure if they had to be spent in a muddy, dull suburbia like New Harmony?

In the past, Paul had made all the decisions. She had respected and adored him too much to find any fault with him. But this time he was wrong, wrong, wrong!

The long taxi ride out to Miriam Denlinger's house helped calm her. There was the music store where she and Jill had listened to records by the hour. There was the soda shop where they had stopped after school. There—yes, there was the concert hall. She leaned toward the window. The posters advertised the next concert—a pianist, playing Chopin. She couldn't miss that. She must find a way to go.

She sank back in the seat, and almost missed seeing the apartment building where they had lived until last June. It was so familiar, so dear that tears sprang to her eyes. The old, distinguished grey stone building, the aged porter at the door, so polite, so kind to the children, the lovely trees in front, the brilliant, lush flower beds kept in immaculate formal beauty.

There must be a way to go back. She must, she would find a way.

Miriam greeted her with delight. "Oh, Susie, Susie, how good to see you again! We've missed you so much! Oh, wait till the girls see you! How wonderful you could come!"

"I wanted to let you know I was coming, but I didn't decide till last night. When I called you, no one answered the phone."

"It doesn't matter—I'm just glad you came! Now come in and tell me everything! How do you like your new house? What about your neighbors? How do the children like their new school?" There was no end to the questions.

Susan was saved by the ringing of the doorbell, but only temporarily. She thought fast, and decided to tell only Jill the truth. If she did not escape soon from New Harmony, they would all feel sorry for her, and she was much too proud to bear that

To the eager questions of the Bridge Club members, she only said lightly, "It's a raw new neighborhood. There's so much work to do that I'm snowed under! Ask me six months from now what I think of it! Living in a house is quite different from apartment living."

They were perceptive enough to see she did not want to discuss it yet, and they were kind enough to turn the conversation to other matters.

Nancy Alter's divorced husband had married his 18-year-old secretary. Nancy had gone on a trip to the Caribbean. The children were in boarding school. They had given up their house—it was too expensive to keep it going. Nancy planned to get a job when she returned.

"I advised her to go," said Miriam. "She was absolutely exhausted, and her nerves were raw. Why does a woman let herself love a man so much? It's asking for trouble."

By the time lunch was ready, five women were there—Miriam, Susan, Jill Ohms, Betty Lorrimer, and a new member, Diana Kirk.

Susan realized she made a fifth for the bridge that would follow. Miriam urged her to play. "I really would rather be hostess, Susan, and you haven't played for ages."

"That's just it," said Susan. "I'm terribly rusty. "And I came in to town more to talk to you than play bridge. Just let me talk to whoever happens to be dummy."

Susan enjoyed the lunch and the conversation that went with it. Miriam served shrimp salad, frozen lima beans, blueberry muffins, and for dessert, strawberry short cake topped with whipped cream. Betty, who was on a diet, moaned with grief.

Jill sat next to Susan. In the distraction provided when Miriam and Diana were teasing Betty, Susan muttered to Jill, "I must talk to you alone. Have to ask—"

Jill's eyes flashed with quick sympathy. "When I'm dummy, we can go out to the kitchen."

Susan nodded, and was silent the rest of the meal, trying to think how to put her complex problem to Jill.

Miriam was dummy first, and they had a talk, then Betty was next. Finally Jill was free, and Jill and Susan moved casually out of the kitchen, ostensibly to get some water.

"You've heard, I suppose, about Paul and Olivia," said Jill abruptly. She reached for a glass, turned on the cold water faucet.

At first Susan did not take in what she had heard, she was so intent on her own questions. "I wanted to ask you—about Paul—" she began; then Jill's words struck home.

"It started before you left Franklin," said Jill bluntly. "I wanted to tell you, but Miriam said to wait, it would blow over."

"Olivia," said Susan blankly.

"Olivia Belgrove is a bitch," said Jill, her cheeks blazing. "She's been divorced twice. I suppose she thinks her money and her social position protect her from any scandal."

Olivia Belgrove. The divorced wife of one of Paul's wealthy customers. Silver-blonde hair, green eyes, an ice-cold manner. And Paul … This was why he was staying in town so much!

"He's—still seeing her?"

"Yes, nights and weekends. That's what you wanted to ask, wasn't it?"

"I wanted—to know," said Susan numbly. Anger would come later. Now she felt frozen, incredulous. Paul—and another woman. How could he? And Susan lived so far from town, he thought she would never find out?

A new throught came. Was this why he had insisted on their moving to New Harmony? Was this why he would not listen to her protests? He wanted her out of the way! He wanted to be free to carry on his affair!

"I'm sorry, Susie," said Jill. "Remember, years ago, we said we'd never lie to each other no matter how much grownups lie?"

"I remember."

"I figured if I knew you—and I do know you—that you would always want to know the truth, no matter how it hurt."

Susan realized she was sitting in a kitchen chair. Jill was still standing beside the sink.

"I'd like a glass of water," said Susan. Jill handed it to her silently.

Susan drank a few swallows. She could not think about Paul's unfaithfulness now. She must get through the rest of the afternoon, take the bus home, be there soon after the children arrived from school. The children. Had Paul considered them at all?

"Susie?" said Jill anxiously.

Susan managed to smile at her with stiff lips. "I'm all right, Jill. Thanks—for telling me. Some friends—wouldn't. But I needed to know that. It explains."

"Yes. If there's anything I can do—"

Susan shook her head. "Not now—not yet. I'll—let you know."

Miriam came out to the kitchen. "We need a fourth," she said gaily, but her eyes were sad, worried, as she looked at Susan.

Susan stood up. "I think I'll go, Miriam," she said, as they walked back to the living room. "The bus takes an hour and a half, and I'd like to be home by the time the children get there."

Jill offered to drive her to the bus, and Susan finally accepted. She kissed them all goodbye.

She had missed them so much. She said so to Jill on the way to the bus.

"We've missed you too," said Jill. "When we went to the concert by ourselves, I wanted to bawl. Paul said you couldn't manage to get in."

"Not just now," said Susan tightly. The coldness was beginning to melt, and she felt a fierce anger blazing up in her.

That Paul should do this to her and the children—for the sake of a woman like Olivia Belgrove?" she asked with assumed lightness. would fight, as she had never fought in all her gentle, peace-loving years.

CHAPTER FOUR

DURING the long bus ride home, her thoughts churned around and around. The cold incredulity gave way to furious anger, then to a frenzy. That Paul could do this to them!

The phone at home rang about five-thirty. It was Paul's part-time secretary, Miss Finch.

"Mr. Wladek asked me to phone, Mrs. Wladek," she said. "He's tied up with a customer for the evening. He decided to stay overnight in town—so he asked me to call you."

Susan stiffened. "Oh. Is the customer Mrs. Belgrove?" she asked with assumed lightness.

There was a long pause. "He didn't say, Mrs. Wladek."

So Miss Finch knew too. Everyone had known about it all along except Susan.

"Thank you for calling," she said coldly.

After she had hung up, she thought of many biting, sarcastic things she could have said. But she did not want to say them to Paul's secretary—only to Paul.

She lay awake half the night, turning restlessly, staring out at the dark sky. What would she say to Paul? She had never questioned him before. His word had always been final. They had never quarreled much until this summer.

She turned again in bed. If she kept silent would the affair "blow over"? Was this one of the humiliating, essential truths a wife had to face? She wondered how Nancy Alter had faced the truth of her husband's affair with his young secretary. She might have blown up, forced the matter into the open. Or she might have lived with it silently, day after day, until it had gone so far that her husband told her he wanted a divorce, because he no longer loved her.

She wished there were no rule of silence on these matters. She did not know what was the wise thing to do. It was hard to think clearly when jealousy raged through her like a green tide of hate, washing away reason.

At this very moment, Paul was probably in bed with Olivia. Perhaps they were awake, pressed close together. Perhaps Paul was kissing her at this very instant—his dark face hot and eager against her white skin.

Susan writhed in fury. Paul had not bothered to make love to her sincerely for years. Love had been a quick, brisk formula, taken at bedtimes to soothe the nerves. She had never protested, never demanded more. Would it have helped if she had? Perhaps Paul also had wanted more love, more affection, more close, tender sexual companionship. Then why hadn't he asked Susan?

Why had he not taken what he wanted from her?

Duane Ackerman came over next morning, and swept the yard.

"It's getting toward winter," he said, when he came into the kitchen. "You can feel the cold in the air today."

She shivered. Winter in this dreadful place—how would they endure it?

She made some chocolate for him. By unspoken agreement, they said nothing about what had happened between them a few days ago. But Susan could not forget it completely, and was sure it was in his mind too.

"Winter," she said. "I suppose it gets awfully cold here. It's so open. There's no shelter, no windbreak."

"Yes. And the snow piles up along the highways. It's bad for the kids going to school."

"I wish I could drive. I hate to think of their walking all winter."

"Don't you drive?"

"No. Paul—" she paused, then went on. "Paul's parents died in an automobile accident. Later he went to live with his aunt and uncle in the country. His aunt was very good to him. Then one day, she was driving to town, and she tried to race a train and get across the tracks. She was killed. Paul never wanted me to drive, so I haven't since we were married.

"But you're sensible! You'd never do a foolish thing like that!"

Susan stared at him. She had always thought Paul was protecting her. She had felt some pride that he was so fond of her he did not want her endangered. Now she realized the truth—Paul thought of her as a fool! He thought she was too incompetent to be allowed to drive!

And he thought she was so stupid that she would make no protest when he moved her out to the country, and then carried on a blatant affair with a woman in town.

Susan felt a new fury. As she finished the dishes, her hands shook with anger. Paul thought she was a fool. Now everything made sense—all his actions that had seemed so incomprehensible.

"Did you enjoy your visit in town, with all your friends?" Duane asked.

She took off her apron, and sat down at the kitchen table with him. "Oh, yes. It was good to see them again."

"Were they all there, Jill, and Nancy, and Betty?"

He had even remembered the names she had mentioned. How serious his green yes were as he looked at her!

"Nancy wasn't there. She's awfully upset about the divorce. She went away to the Caribbean with some friends. When she comes back, she's going to get a job."

"I don't see how a guy could do that. I mean, love a woman and marry her, and have kids. Then just like that, he decides he loves his secretary. I don't see it."

"Men are like that," said Susan bitterly. "They can love a woman, then turn around and hurt her so badly—"

"I never would," said Duane. "Boy, I never would. I hate hurting anything, even mice. I'd never hurt a person."

She put her fingers on his big muscular hand. "I don't think you would. You're so kind."

Duane put his other hand over hers, and for a moment she let him hold it. Her hand felt safe and warm inside his. He cared for her, quietly, undemandingly. He thought more of her than Paul did—Paul, who had slept with another woman last night.

Susan stood up and carried the chocolate cup over to the sink, rinsed it out. She was aware of Duane watching her, not possessively, not boldly, but with affection and desire.

"Do you have a girl friend, Duane?" she asked idly.

"Gee, no."

"I'll bet you do, and you just won't tell me. You ought to be with her, not with an old woman like me."

"You aren't old. You're young—and awful pretty."

"I guess I was fishing for that." She turned to face him.

"You are pretty. But you're better than pretty. Your eyes light up when you talk. And you know so many things I never heard before—like that music." Duane nodded toward the record player in the living room. The music was flowing on, an undercurrent to their talk.

"I love music. It's necessary to me," she said. He was listening with flattering attention. "I need music, and art, and beauty, and love. Those are the really important things in life, I think. Not so much the food and elaborate clothes. Fur coats—who needs a fur coat? But music! I can't live without it. Something in me would curl up and die."

"Music—art—and love. I like that," he said. His face was shining with pleasure. "Wish I knew how to live that way."

She felt like teasing him again. "Well, you have love anyhow. I'll bet your girl friend sees to that. You're a good-looking boy."

He flushed red again. "I told you before, I don't have a girl. I've never—I never did make love to a woman in my life. I wouldn't know how to go about it."

"You mean, you've never gone to bed with a woman? I thought boys always managed somehow—"

He went even redder. "No! I mean I haven't even kissed one! Gosh, I don't know what you think! But I'd be scared even to kiss one."

"Why, Duane, I'm surprised at you. A girl would be proud to have you for a boy friend. And you're hanging back."

"I just don't know how to act—how to kiss a girl. The girls around here think a lot about kissing. In cars and such. But I don't have a car, and even if I did I wouldn't know what girl to ask. They're—some of them are sort of hard, if you know what I mean. Not soft and pretty, like you."

Impulsively, she went over to him where sat beside the table, and bent to his lips. A sudden warmth went through her at the touch. It had been so long since Paul had embraced her...She was so lonely, starved for love—

His hands clutched her waist, pulled her closer. She kissed him again, because he was hungry for kisses, and she had been deprived too long herself. Then, without knowing how it happened, she found herself sitting on his knees, held in a strong awkward clasp, as he kissed her lips, her cheeks, her ears, in blind desperate caresses.

"Duane," she said faintly. He held her more tightly. She wanted to struggle, to pull away, but instead she went limp against him, let him go on fondling and kissing her.

"I want to love you, I want you," he was muttering.

"I want it too," she said with sudden desperation. "Come into my room."

"Now?"

"Yes."

He let her up and stood, his face glowing, enchanted. She drew him with her and they crossed the living room slowly, arms around each other. In her room, he sat on the bed and watched her, frankly curious, as she undressed with care before him.

The rain was pouring in wild torrents, and the wind rattled against the windows. It was chilly in Susan's room. She got under the covers and waited for him. He undressed hastily, awkwardly, piling his clothes on a chair. Then he got in with her, and she felt his long lean-muscled body stretching beside hers.

He was awkward and unsure. He did not know what to do. Gently tenderly, she guided him through the preliminary love play.

"Kiss me first, a lot more," she urged. She encouraged him to touch her, but his hands were timid on her breasts. She ran her fingers through his curly hair, caressed his head and neck, drew him down to kiss his lips. She liked the taste of his mouth. It was young and hard and eager. He learned swiftly, became bolder with his hands and body.

She smiled at the delightful luxury of the long lovemaking. Paul was often hasty and perfunctory, getting his satisfaction, rolling over to go to sleep at once.

Duane was pressing eagerly, uncertainly against her. He wanted to go on. She was ready too. She led him on gently.

He was as curious as he was ardent, and wanted to know why about everything. She explained, patiently, but her body was roused to a keen pitch, and she wanted him badly.

This was his first time, and she wanted it to be perfect for him. She held him to slow movements, directed him with her hands and voice, then when he understood, she lay back and let him go on as he wished. Through half-open eyes she watched him, his intent face, his lean shoulders, his tanned chest. Then she felt his oneness with her, and she forgot his newness to her for a while in her own intense pleasure.

She caught hold of him as he moved. "That's it—more—more—" He was, for a few minutes, only the instrument of her joy. The delightful fullness was rising in her, the painful stretching, then the delicious adjusting, the fierce thrusting and the wilful retreating.

Then he paused. She wondered, waiting, as he pressed his lips against her, pushing aside her breasts to caress below her breasts, his hands rubbing her, moving over her stomach and hips. He half raised up, moving back the blankets, to look at her with wide adoring eyes, staring at her with new awareness. She felt naked under his gaze as she had never felt, open and revealed to a man as though he owned her and knew her. He was inside her and outside her, over her with his body, under her with his hands under her hips pressing them together.

She felt possessed and stripped under the candid gaze of this boy. What did he think? Did the sight of her please him completely? Did he like her full breasts, sagging a little, with the rosy points hard? He bent down again, pressing his length of body against her chilled body, and the warmth flowed from him to her, heating her, rousing her wildly to fulfillment.

"Duane—"

She shivered heavily, and clutched at him. She meant to tell him to stop before the end, but it was too late. He was crashing against her, filling her, his fulfillment following hers closely. It was too late and she did not care. It was so delicious to feel him shivering in her arms, convulsed against her as she was convulsed under him. He was crying out, and hugging and crushing her. Then he fell down against her, his head helpless on her breast. She kissed him and whispered to him.

"It was wonderful, Duane. Just right. So lovely, so right. Oh, didn't you like it too? Didn't you, my darling?" He was heavy on her, but she loved it, and held him tightly there.

It took him a while to recover. She reminded herself it was his first time, and caressed and soothed him. He moved to lie beside her, and she bent over him, and touched his face and chest with tender hands. His eyes were closed. He might have been lifeless except for the rapid rise and fall of his chest. Finally his eyes opened and he gazed up at her in wonder and awe. She smiled down at him, then bent and brushed his chest with her mouth, in a long slow kiss.

"Are you all right, darling?" she asked. She was concerned about him.

"Fine. Fine," he whispered. He was still gazing at her.

"Did you like it? Or did you—" she hesitated. Surely he had not hated it. He must have enjoyed it too. Yet he might have been too shocked, or surprised.

"Oh, yes, Oh, yes. I've never been so happy in my life." He reached up, gravely, and touched the point of her breast with his forefinger.

She glanced at the clock. Only 10:30. They could lie here for two hours... but maybe they should not.

He answered her look. "I'd like to stay a while."

She nodded and lay down at his side. He turned, looking at her. Then he dared to put his hand on her again, to touch her curiously and feel her. Susan stretched lazily. She felt so good! She had wanted this; it had given her a wonderful sense of release.

Now that the storm was no longer raging inside her, she could hear the records, still playing. She teased Duane by beating the time of the music on his chest and his shoulders, then, as he drew her closer, on his back. He hugged her tight.

"Is that the way people always make love?" he wanted to know.

"No. There are many ways."

"Tell me about some."

She told him as much as she could. He listened. "Which way do you like best?"

She was surprised to her herself say, "I think I'm learning as much as you are."

He smiled in quick delight. "I like that—" and reached for her.

She moved into his arms with the feeling of entering delight and forgetfulness. Their bodies twined together and they met easily and fully. She lay and felt his hand caressing her, as their bodies adjusted to each other, and she could no longer remember any problems or worries. The world had disappeared, and in this room was the only reality, a man's hard body meeting her soft one, and each guiding the other to rich ecstasy.

CHAPTER FIVE

A defiant, guilty happiness lingered with Susan over the next two days. Paul had treated her callously—deserted her. Well, she would find her pleasure elsewhere. She had a right to some happiness in this world!

Duane had been overwhelmingly grateful. He had adored her with his hands, with his serious boyish eyes, his stammered words. She had no regrets. She had given the boy a beautiful experience that he would never forget. His sober face had glowed with incredulous joy that day.

She knew deep inside that what they had done was wrong, but her body had admitted no such moral reproof. It had felt alive, on fire, wild, then deliciously satisfied, for the first time in years—since the early years of her marriage.

What had gone wrong with their marriage, that it had come to this strangeness and barrier between herself and Paul? She pondered it, but could not find the answer. Paul was acting coldly, cruelly, for no reason she could comprehend.

When Pam and Harvey came home from school that Friday afternoon, Pam was obviously upset.

"What's the matter?" asked Susan, worried again about the children and their adjustment to New Harmony.

"Aw, she has to have a boy friend!" said Harvey in disgust, pulling off his jacket.

"I do not! That isn't so!" Pam started to cry, and flopped down on the sofa.

"What do you mean? Why does she have to have a boy friend? She's only twelve." Susan felt exasperated by this new development.

"There's a school dance," said Pam tearfully.

"Well, we can take you. You don't have to have a boy friend."

"Yes, I do. You can't go unless you have a date," sobbed Pam. "And nobody asked me! All the girls have dates, but nobody asked me."

"In the seventh grade!" Susan was still incredulous.

Duane was standing nearby. He nodded. "That's the way they do it here. Group dances in fourth, fifth, and sixth grades, dating in seventh and on up."

"Good grief! And I suppose they're married by the time they're in high school!"

"Lots are," said Duane. "Kids grow up fast around here."

She caught his eye and blushed, thinking of the session in her bedroom. Duane himself had grown up, fast.

"But what am I going to do?" wailed Pam. "If I start out wrong, if I don't get a date for the first dance, I'm finished! I might as well not live here at all!"

Susan wanted to answer tartly that it would be much better if none of them lived here. But that was something to be fought out with Paul.

"Well, let me think," she said. "Is there any boy you know who isn't dated up already?"

Pam shook her head, her black hair flying about her tear-stained cheeks.

"What about Merv Weston?" asked Duane.

"Merv!" said Pam. "He wouldn't go to a dance!"

"He's a good kid," said Duane. "Now listen, is it better to go with someone like Merv, or not go at all?"

Pam sniffed back more tears. "He—he won't ask me."

"I'll fix it up if you want. He'd be scared to ask you if he thought you'd turn him down. If I get him to call you, will you say yes?"

Pam nodded. "But I hope nobody finds out it was fixed up."

"Gee, I hope I never get to seventh grade," said Harvey, and went out to the kitchen for an apple.

Pam ran upstairs. Susan thanked Duane. "It's good of you to bother. But what is all this—dating in the seventh grade?"

"The kids start earlier all the time. A lot of them marry and quit high school. Of course, about half of them get divorces within a few years. It's rough on the kids. Someone ought to stop them, I think. The laws ought to be tougher if the parents won't do anything."

"What else can you expect, when they date so early? But Pam—I don't want that for her. I want her to go to college."

"If she lives around here, she won't," said Duane. "Nobody around here goes to college. They get married and work, that's all."

"Say, Duane." Harvey had wandered in from the kitchen. "Do you know how to fight?"

"Well—some, I guess. Why?"

"Now, Harvey, I don't want you fighting."

"I have to, Mom," he said, gazing at her with his calm brown eyes, so like Paul's. "See, there's this gang. They say if I learn to fight, I can get in. I have to be able to fight kids my own age."

"But, Harvey!" Susan wailed. "I don't want you in a gang!"

"Around here, you're in a gang, or you're out of a gang and the gang fights you. I'll have to learn to fight, either way. Can you teach me, huh, Duane?"

"I guess so." Duane looked at Susan to see her reaction. "All right?"

"I suppose it has to be—for the present. All right."

Duane took Harvey outside, and began instructing him in the art of self-defense. Susan winced as she heard the blows, the grunts.

Pam came down to the kitchen. "Say, what's going on out there?"

"Duane is teaching Harvey how to fight," said Susan bitterly.

"Good idea," said Pam. "Around here, all anybody cares about is fighting and making love."

"What?" Susan's face felt scorched.

"And money," Pam added moodily. "Nobody cares about music, or concerts, or art. One girl told me not to talk about art, or people would think I was being snooty."

"What girl was that?"

Pam hesitated. "Her name is Coral Emmert. She's in eighth grade. She flunked once. She's awfully popular."

"Flunked!"

"Yes. She doesn't think much about grades. She says other things in life are more important, like clothes and boys."

Duane and Harvey talked during their training sessions. Before Duane went home at five-thirty, he stopped in the kitchen to see Susan.

"That gang he wants in—it's Fred Goss's gang. Some of the gangs aren't so bad. Just kids messing around. But Goss—I don't know about him."

"Who is he, Duane?"

"His father runs a factory a couple miles north of town. He hires a lot of people from New Harmony, and he's on the City Council. He's a big man around here, and people don't like to step on his son's toes."

"What about his mother? What kind of a woman is she?"

"She's dead. She committed suicide about three years ago."

"Suicide!"

"Yes. Goss had a woman. Everybody knew it. Then this woman, she had a baby. I guess Mrs. Goss couldn't take any more. Old man Goss has a mean streak, they say. And he thinks he can get away with anything, account of his money."

"Oh, the poor woman. And what about the boy?"

"Oh, Fred runs around with his convertible—he's sixteen, so it's legal now, but he'd had a car since he was thirteen. He runs his gang the way his old man runs his factory—egging on guys to fight each other for high place."

Paul finally came home that night, cross and tired. When Susan said she wanted to talk to him, he growled, "Tomorrow. I don't want any more tonight! I'm fed to the teeth with problems!"

She bit her lip, but finally said, "All right. Tomorrow, then."

She went to bed alone in the spare room that was her own bedroom now. She lay awake a long time planning what she would say to Paul.

It took a while to decide, but she finally made up her mind that if she wanted to get the children away from New Harmony, she must not mention Paul's affair. This was no time to bring it up. Perhaps there never would be a time to confront him with her knowledge.

It was a bitter pill to swallow, but she knew that first of all she must get the children back to Franklin, to safety. Maybe by that time, Paul would be tired of Olivia and ready to end the affair. Olivia, thought Susan, was a shallow woman, who had married for money, and divorced to get a large settlement. She would not be interested for long in an immigrant importer who had to work hard for his moderate income.

Paul slept late Saturday morning. After breakfast, he worked in the yard. Susan was glad to have him do the work, but she felt he was avoiding her. She was sure of it when he stayed outdoors until lunch, then after lunch announced that he was tired and was going to sleep all afternoon.

She let him go, grimly. She would have a talk with him this weekend. He could not avoid her forever!

Paul took them to a movie, at a town ten miles away, on Saturday evening. Susan wanted to point out how far they had to go to find entertainment. But the children were so happy to go out with their father, to have him paying a little attention to them again, that she would not spoil their pleasure.

Paul slept late again on Sunday, waking only in time to take the family to church. Pamela and Harvey recognized several children from school. Susan saw no one she knew except the minister, who was cordial and greeted them by name.

Paul remarked, as they drove away from church, "As dry as usual! Churches nowadays don't have much life to them."

Susan, who had felt calmed and inspired by the simple service and the prayers, decided again that she and Paul had drawn miles apart from each other.

She served a large Sunday dinner. She and Pam did the dishes while Paul and Harvey played ball.

Paul came in while Susan was finishing the pans. "Susan, I am tired enough to sleep some more, I think. This fresh country air is wonderful."

After he went to bed, Pam said, "Fresh country air! He should get a whiff of the stink from sewers we walk past on the way to school."

So Paul was avoiding her! Susan finished in the kitchen, took off her apron, and straightened her hair by the mirror on the pantry door. Her hands were trembling. She was afraid of Paul, of his anger. But she must control herself. She must be calm and sure, or Paul would not listen. Emotion was weakness.

Pam was reading in the front room. Harvey was playing ball by himself in the yard.

Susan went to Paul's bedroom. The door was closed. After a brief hesitation, she knocked.

"Come in!" he called. Susan opened the door. Paul was stretched out on the bed. "Susan! You honor me. You haven't bothered to come in here for quite some time."

"I have to talk to you," she said, ignoring his sarcasm. She had no intention of letting him bait her into any lovemaking. If Duane had not satisfied her, she might have been tempted, but now she knew she could resist easily.

"Come in. Sit down." Paul patted the bed beside him and grinned at her. He could be charming when he wanted to.

She sat down in a chair near the window. He raised his eyebrows mockingly, his dark eyes shining with mirth.

"Are you angry with me?" he asked.

"No," she said. "But I've got to talk to you about the children." She told him about the seventh-grade dance, Pam's date. Then she told about Harvey's fighting.

"Good for him! I approve. He's always been too much an introvert."

"It's not the fighting itself I object to," she explained patiently. "But this gang may be vicious. I don't want Harvey involved with a bunch of juvenile delinquents."

"Nonsense! They don't have juvenile delinquency out here in the country. That's the main reason I wanted to move—for the children's sake. The country air is good for them too. Harvey has a good tan, and he plays a much better game of ball than before. You should see to it that Pam gets outside too. You say she has a date for the dance."

"Yes. Duane arranged it. But she—"

"Good. I want her to be popular. Pam has always been too shy. Yes, I think this move was a smart thing." He stretched, yawning, and closed his eyes.

Susan stared at him helplessly. He had taken all her arguments and twisted them to his own use. "But, Paul, you don't understand! This town is all wrong for them. I don't want Harvey involved in a gang, or Pam going with boys when she's so young. It isn't good—it isn't wholesome."

"Don't be a fool," he said sleepily. "You've just proved that it is. Harvey is learning to get along with other boys. Pam is coming out of her shell. I would think—" he opened his eyes and looked at her—"you're the only one who is not happy here."

"Me?" she asked faintly.

"Yes. You were coming along well enough until you went to talk with those bridge friends of yours. They've made you dissatisfied. I'll bet you miss them a lot! Your Wednesday luncheons, your bridge, your concerts, your socials—Yes, you're the one who wants to move back to town. Well, I won't let Pam and Harvey grow up like that."

The attack was so contrary to what she expected that she felt confused. She had forgotten how Paul attacked, how the fighter in him found the weakness of the other side, and probed it until there was nothing to do but fall back on the defensive.

"Paul, it isn't just that. I miss them, yes, but I'm thinking of the children."

"You're thinking about yourself. And why not? You are a very attractive woman." Paul sat up. "Come to bed," he said. "We have not made love for a long time."

"No, Paul, I don't want—"

"You will. Come on." He was smiling, looking straight at her. She felt weak, ready to give in. Oh, she was a spineless creature, she thought. She knew he had spent recent nights with Olivia, yet when she looked at him, his long legs stretched out on the bed, his hand held out to her invitingly, she wanted him again.

She stood up. Paul misunderstood, and moved over to make room for her. She retreated to the door. "I—I have to help Pam," she stammered.

Paul frowned. "You mean you want your own way, and until you get it you will not make love! You are a cold woman. Love is not to bargain with!"

"I know," said Susan. "And it isn't something to be held back, and then handed out as a reward for good behavior!"

Paul stared after her. She closed the door, and fled to the kitchen. She despised herself for wishing she had stayed. And she had not won the argument—she had not even succeeded in arguing her case fully. Paul was too clever for her.

CHAPTER SIX

ONE of the many problems of being without a car in a large, sprawling town like New Harmony was the problem of getting groceries. Susan walked to the shopping center two or three times a week, and carried home heavy armloads. The mile home often seemed more like five. For the first couple of months, Paul had been around to help, but now he could not be depended upon to be there in the evenings or on weekends.

Duane tried to help her, but he was too tired, at the end of his long, hard day, and she hated to have him walk that distance with her groceries in addition to his own. She had ordered a shopping cart in Franklin, but it had not arrived yet. Even with the cart, getting groceries and supplies this winter would be a difficult problem.

On Monday, Susan found she had an unusually large grocery list, so she asked Pam and Harvey to meet her at the shopping center after school and help her bring things home. Then, about two-thirty she walked the mile to the center.

She went to the drug store first, then to the miniature department store. She had an armful of packages before she went to the grocery.

Duane saw her as she entered, and hurried over with a shopping cart. He looked different from the boy she knew, in his white clerk's outfit, a pencil behind his ear.

"Put these in the bottom section of the cart," he said, and helped her unload her bundles. "You can't carry all these, not all that way home."

"Pam and Harvey are going to meet me after school."

"Oh, that's good." His face showed immediate relief. "Now, what else do you need?"

"I can find everything. Don't bother—you have work to do."

He hesitated, looking around the busy store. The clerks at the check-out counters each had a line of customers. "Guess you're right. But let me know if you want anything you can't find."

"All right." She pushed the cart over to the far aisle and started along the rows of canned goods. She should have had Paul bring her to the grocery on Saturday—but had not been able to think of anything but the frantic need to escape from the trap they were all in.

How far away she felt from the ordered harmony and calm life in Franklin! There, she had walked two blocks to her neighborhood shopping area, and had sent home the groceries and drugs she needed. Everyone had known her—the butcher had saved choice cuts of fresh meat, the grocery clerk helped her pick the best vegetables; she never had to worry about carrying large bundles. On the way home she often stopped at the bakery for piping hot rolls, fresh bread, cookies, cake made that morning.

Here everything was packaged, or frozen, or processed to last a long time. She supposed that was necessary, but oh, how she missed the fresh, unprocessed flavor of the old ways! Progress, she thought bitterly. They take the flavor and vitamins out of bread, and add chemicals to make it seem fresh when it isn't— and that's progress.

It was past three-fifteen by the time she had finished her hasty marketing. Duane came over to her as she headed for the check-out line. He helped her unload the packages on the counter. It looked like a huge amount of groceries, but she knew the food would not last long in their family.

The clerk added busily. The cash register rang and rang again, with a noisy emphatic sound that jarred on Susan's ears.

Everything seemed to irritate her these days. She felt as thought she had been flung out of a beautiful, ordered, meaningful life into a chaotic, senseless existence in which one had to fight to stay alive. She resented the change deeply. It was so unnecessary, so cruel!

The door swung open near her, and a woman dashed in. "Those kids, those horrible kids!" she panted. "They're fighting again! Someone ought to stop them!"

The woman clerk shrugged, didn't bother to look up. "The kids are always fighting," she said. "Twenty-two dollars and fifty-six cents."

Susan gasped in surprise. It was even more than she had expected. She paid it, and waited while Duane and the clerk packed her groceries in bags.

A small crowd had gathered at the windows. "Look at them," one woman said. "It's disgusting! Someone ought to stop it."

It was about time for Pam and Harvey to come. Susan did not want them to get involved in a fight.

"I'd better go out and wait for the children at the other end of the parking lot," she told Duane. "I don't want them to go through that crowd."

"I'll help you carry your things," he said. They piled the cart full and he wheeled it to the entrance. Susan glanced anxiously at the growing crowd outside. There were some big boys there. They were huddled around a small ring, in which some smaller children were struggling.

"Pam!" screamed Susan. It was Pam's red tam she saw, and her plaid coat. "It's Pam!" She dropped her bundles on the floor of the grocery and ran outside.

Duane yelled back at another man. "Call the police!" Then he ran after her.

Susan fought her way into the crowd of yelling, taunting boys. "Get him! Kick him! Pull her hair!"

She shoved them out of her path with the violent strength of fear. By the time she reached the center of the ring, Duane was close behind her.

"Pam!" she cried. "Pam!"

The girl in the red tam was struggling to free herself from the grip of two older boys, who held her, and laughed as she struggled. Another girl stood in front of her, slapping her face with regular hard blows of her open palms. Pam's eyes were shut, her face streaked with angry red marks where she had been hit.

"Mom!" cried Harvey. "Look out!"

She saw Harvey kicking wildly at one of the boys who held Pam. He was being pulled away by another big boy, but he was putting up a wild struggle. Nearby, two other small children were being hit by older ones.

Susan screamed at the boys who held Pam, "Let her go! Let her go!" She grabbed the girl who was hitting Pam and flung her away, then struck one of the boys holding Pam. "Let her go, you little animal!" She gave him a kick with her foot, and he let Pam go, howling in pain.

"Look out, Mom!" Harvey yelled again. "Duane, get that guy!"

Susan felt someone strike at her from behind. She ducked away, hit a gangling boy, knocking him down, and turned to see Duane. Other boys surged forward. She saw the grinning, excited faces of the boys, and girls, too, who closed in around her and the children. She flung her arms around Pam to protect her. Harvey was putting up a futile fight against three boys now.

Sirens. Shrieking shrill wails of sirens. A police car was driving up to them, across the parking lot. The crowd melted away—boys ran in every direction.

By the time the police had jumped out of the car, only the smaller children, Susan and Duane were left.

"What's going on here?" one policeman demanded.

"I don't know. My children—beaten up—" said Susan hysterically.

Harvey said, "They followed us—after school. They—said they'd—beat us up—Don't know—why—except we—don't belong—" He was panting with rage, out of breath from fighting. Mud streaked his face and his clothes. He had lost his cap. His sweater was torn half off.

Pam was in worse condition. Her dress was torn and muddy, her coat ripped, her face scratched and bleeding, her blue eyes dazed with shock. Harvey had met the attack with anger, and it had helped save him. Shy, trusting Pam had been so stunned she had scarcely been able to fight back, and now she was shaking with nervous tremors, unable to speak.

Susan held her in her arms, tried to soothe her. Duane was talking to the policeman, and to several women who had ventured out of the store. The police took the three small children with them, and left. Duane came back to Susan.

"Aren't they going to take out statements? Aren't they going to arrest those boys?" Susan demanded.

Duane said, with a flare of anger, "It happens every day. They said they couldn't do anything unless you want to press charges. They don't usually arrest boys for this, and they don't advise you to swear out warrants. It's nothing to take to court, they said."

"It isn't? And it happens every day! My God, what kind of a town is this?" Susan was appalled. "Aren't the police going to do anything?"

"They're as helpless as we are," said a woman who had come up beside them. "I complain and complain, but the kids just get worse. If their parents won't stop them, nobody else can. They're spoiled rotten."

"This is Mrs. Weston," said Duane. "Mrs. Weston, Mrs. Wladek."

"How do you do?" said Susan.

"I'll take you home," said Mrs. Weston. "I live down your way, and it just isn't safe to walk. You ought to have a car."

Susan accepted her offer gratefully. She and Duane got the groceries, then the children and she piled into Mrs. Weston's car and rode home. They went past the house with the goldfish pond.

"That's my house," said Mrs. Weston. "I've tried to fix it up, but I guess I'm not much good at prettying things."

She was a small, thin woman, sparked with a driving nervous energy. Susan wondered how she liked New Harmony—if she endured it because she wanted to stay here, or if her husband was the one who wanted to stay.

At their house, Susan tried to thank her.

"Oh, don't mention it! I'm glad to help. Besides, I've wanted to get acquainted. My Mervin is real fond of your Pamela." She smiled brightly.

"Oh—oh, yes," said Susan. Pam hadn't said a word. "Well, thank you again."

"I'll see you sometime! Let me know if you want me to help out with groceries, or whatever."

"Thank you." She wanted to be more gracious, but she felt as though she had been knocked over the head. She wanted only to get in the house and shut the door on this horrible world.

Harvey and Susan carried the groceries into the house. Pam came in, and walked to her room like a sleepwalker, her town dress flopping about her knees.

"I'll put these away, Mom. You go see if Pam's okay," said Harvey. He seemed much older than nine just then. "I'm going to get more fighting lessons from Duane. Next time, I'll get them good."

"While three of them hold you? How can you fight animals like that?" asked Susan bitterly. "They don't fight fair. They're beasts, cowards, fighting only when they can win easily, picking on children much smaller than they are."

Harvey didn't reply. His face was set in hard, mature lines. Susan went upstairs to find Pam.

She found her daughter lying face down across her bed, her coat and hat on the floor. It was not like Pam to be so careless, but Susan did not blame her. She sat down on the bed beside the girl, and put her hand on her shoulders. Pam was stiff, tense.

"Darling, I'm so sorry, so sorry. Let me see your face. Did that girl—" Her voice broke. Pam turned over so Susan could see her face. It was swollen and bruised, marked with deep scratches.

"She wanted to hurt me, because I was pretty. She did it to hurt me." Pam's voice was stifled, barely audible.

Susan got antiseptics and cleaned her face carefully. Pam submitted to her ministrations docilely, but her mind was still reeling under the shock of the attack.

"Why did she, Mom? Why did the boys hold me and let her hit me?"

"I don't know, darling. I think they're jealous of you. And they're spoiled. They think they can hit anybody and get away with it."

"Yes, they can. The police don't even stop them, do they?"

"No. They don't seem to."

"It's because Harvey and me aren't in a gang. If you're in a gang, they don't dare touch you."

"I don't want you in one of those gangs! They're vicious, they're terrible—"

"But when you're in the gang, you don't get beaten up."

"There are better ways to solve this. I'm going to speak to your father."

"He won't do anything."

Susan stared at Pam. Pam had never said anything like that before. She had always adored her father.

"Yes, he will! He must!"

"He doesn't want us to leave. That's the only way we can get away from those kids. I guess Harvey and I will have to figure out what to do."

Her blue eyes were distant, guarded. She said no more.

CHAPTER SEVEN

PAUL was late getting home that night. He was tired and irritable as he always was these days. This time Susan ignored his scowl, and proceeded to tell him in detail about the attack on Pam and Harvey.

He went to see Pam. Susan had put her to bed and given her supper on a tray. He was not long in coming back.

"Her face looks bad, but she says it's all right. She's quite calm. Really, Susan, you get upset over anything these days."

"Anything! I don't call it just anything to have the children held by force and beaten by children several years older!"

"Children always tease and torment the new students. When they get acquainted, they will all calm down and be friends. I remember when I was a boy, and moved to the country outside Warsaw, the first day of school was one fight after the other."

Susan lost her temper and screamed at him. "Do you think that's all it was? A fight between a couple of kids? Well, it wasn't! Two boys held Pamela, your daughter, held her while she was struck over and over again! They struck me! And Harvey was kicked and hit by several boys! And the police did nothing! Nothing!"

"Don't raise your voice!"

Susan began to sob. She sat down at the dining room table and wept. "Oh, I don't know how to make you see! You're being so pigheaded—This wasn't a clean fight! The children didn't have a chance, not a chance!"

"Stop crying! My God, you make more of it than Pam and Harvey. Stop it, Susan!"

She could not stop crying. Her rage, her futile, helpless feeling at the indifference of her husband, her shock and reaction from the violent scene of the afternoon, made her hysterical.

"You don't care about them, or me! You're gone all week. You don't care what happens—"

"For the love of God, don't start that! I work all week, remember? I work in an office to earn money to buy your food and clothes, and this house! Understand?"

"This house!' she wept. "This house—that we don't want! This horrible house in this horrible place—"

"This is your gratitude! I work myself half to death, and what do you care! Well, by God, we are here in this house, and here we stay! You're not going to get me out with your tricks and your crying!"

He went out, slamming the door. She heard the car start, and he drove away.

Harvey said, from the doorway, "Mom, don't cry any more. We'll manage, all right."

He came over and patted her shoulder awkwardly. She started crying afresh, and finally went to bed, to lie awake, scared, appalled, desperately trying to find a way out.

In the morning, Paul curtly informed her he was staying in town overnight. He had packed a suitcase large enough for a week, and left early without breakfast.

Pam came in to breakfast, dressed for school. Her face was swollen and bruised, her blue eyes dazed. She seemed unnaturally calm. Susan tried to persuade her not to go to school.

"I'd better, Mom. It's worse if you try to hide. I'd better go."

She went off with Harvey. Susan watched them from the window, her heart heavy. She was a poor fighter. She had not helped her children at all. Paul had failed them—and she was failing them too. She just was not strong enough, clever enough, intelligent enough, to fight their battles and win.

Duane came over soon after the children had left. "How were they this morning?" he asked.

Susan shook her head. "I wanted them to stay home. Pam said it would only make things worse. Oh, Duane, what am I going to do?"

She felt the weak tears coming again, and pulled out her handkerchief, turning her back to him.

"I know how you feel," he said. "I wish I could do their fighting for them, but I can't."

"Will it be better if they get into a gang? Harvey seems to think so. But I hate for them to join one."

"You don't join one. You get taken in, or left out. It's all up to them. Well, I don't know. If they stay around here, they'll be better all in a gang than outside."

She turned. He was standing beside the table, looking at her. There was hunger on his face. But he would not demand love from her.

She walked back to him, put her hands on his shoulders, and pressed her body against his hard lean body. He loved her, he wanted her. And her hurt spirit wanted an unquestioning love, an affection that was soothing and gentle.

His arms closed about her, holding her close. She lifted her face for his kisses. His mouth touched her cheeks, then came hotly to her lips, opened against her mouth.

The fire blazed out swiftly between them. Their mouths were open, clinging, their tongues searching. She let her head fall back against his arm, yielding her body limply to his use.

He held her more tightly, crushing her against him. He wanted her now. She could feel his readiness, his need.

She drew her head away for a moment. "Let's go—to my room—" she murmured.

He started. She could feel the jerk of his body so close to hers.

"Will you—will you—"

"Yes."

They went to her room silently. Her heart was pounding so loudly that she felt deafened. She had meant to undress, as she had before. But he was impatient, his self-control slipping away.

He pushed her down across the bed, then fumbled quickly with her clothes, delighted with her femaleness.

He fell across her, eagerly, blunderingly, hotly anxious for the meeting.

She let him do as he pleased. The thin young body crouched over her. He clung to her with trembling eagerness. She curved up lovingly to him, holding him gently with her hands on his thin waist.

It was over too soon. He lay back, sighing. She got up, after a few minutes, to undress. He sat up on the bed.

"Don't go!" he begged. "Don't go yet. I want—I want you so much."

She smiled at him, and slipped off her dress. "I'm not going anywhere," she said.

He relaxed and smiled, his sober face crinkling up with pleasure as he watched her. When she was naked, he got up and, still dressed himself, held her with his hands. They stood there, pressed against each other, kissing absorbedly, her body cool under his seeking fingers.

Then he let her lie down again on the bed while he undressed. He saw her watching him, and smiled again, and stood boldly for her to see him. He was different from what he had been in their first meeting. He was more sure of himself now, more confident.

After some moments, he sat down on the bed, and looked at her closely. She wondered at him. He touched her lips, played with them, smoothing them, pressing her cheeks with his fingers, pinching her teasingly.

She was beginning to be deeply aroused. She lay still, eyes heavy, waiting for him. But he wanted to play with her. He bent over her, kissed her marvelingly—bit her softly.

Then he lowered his head, touching her, stroking over her, kissing her body with slow open-mouthed kisses.

She stirred, wanting him now. Still he made her wait. He wanted to look at her, with youthful curiosity, growing boldness. He explored her as even her husband had not done, experimenting with her reactions to his kisses, his touch on exquisitely sensitive places.

She murmured, "Duane!" She felt she ought to protest.

He said, "If you don't like it—if I'm doing something wrong—"

"No," she sighed with luxurious pleasure. "Go on. Go on, darling."

He took her permission as a license to find his extravagant pleasure in her. His kisses lingered, he drew back only to look at her with fascinated interest. But looking and touching were not enough. In each other they had found reality. That was what mattered.

He lay down beside her, and drew her to him. She smiled as she let her body blend smoothly with his.

Time lost it meaning.

She felt curiously justified. This house had always felt strange to her, not as it ought to be—not a place of happiness.

She had a right to happiness with Duane...

How sweet he was, how good to her! If Paul had shown one tenth of Duane's thoughtfulness—but she wouldn't think of Paul now. She would shut him out of her mind.

She had a sense of ecstacy, cried out, held him tightly, as the wild pleasure overwhelmed her, then lay limp on him. She recovered to the feel of his gentle hands on her body, smoothing over her. How good it felt, not to be thrust away at the end, not to be left alone! This boy understood already how a woman felt, how she wanted to be caressed, even after the embrace was finished.

How did he know? Perhaps love had given him the knowledge, love and his own deep need for love.

She fell asleep against him as he held her. She had lain awake too long last night. She slept for a while, then wakened to find him bending over her, watching her sleep.

"Oh. What time is it?" she muttered.

"Twelve-fifteen. Shall I go?"

"Whatever you want."

"I want to stay."

She smiled, and stretched luxuriously under his intent gaze. She ended the stretch of her arms with her hands on his shoulders, and drew him down again to her.

He stayed until after two. They made love again and again, wildly, recklessly.

"You'll be too tired to work tonight," she said at last, after a frenzied embrace.

"I don't care. I love you. I love you." He pressed his mouth against hers.

She was startled by his words, shocked and surprised. Love! Yes, she knew he adored her with a boyish passion. He thought it was love.

When he had finally left, she dressed, and went back to the living room. She saw him leave his house to go to work, and answered his wave. He walked to work whistling. She heard the whistle several moments after he had disappeared down the highway. Then it was silent.

Love. Duane loved her. He was not angry at anyone, jealous of anyone. He did not use her for his pleasure or to have revenge on someone else.

She felt ashamed of herself. Paul had betrayed her, and she was angry with him. But it was not right to drag this boy into their quarrel, to punish him for Paul's wrongdoing. And no matter how much he had enjoyed their lovemaking, he would be hurt by her eventually.

It must not happen again. She must not be so weak and foolish, ever again. If she could not be strong for her own sake, then she must be strong for Duane. He would be hurt if she let him keep on like this.

What had happened to her? Here she was a woman of thirty-three, letting a boy of eighteen make love to her. Letting him? No, encouraging, attracting, enticing him. Begging him for more, more, more, because she was so starved for love.

This had to stop. Today must be the last time she lost her head. She must not let his sweetness, his tenderness betray her into hurting him.

After school was out, she waited at the window for the children to come home. As the minutes dragged by, she became more and more anxious. She was on the verge of calling the police when she finally saw them coming. They were walking along slowly, talking.

Harvey waved his hands in the air, talking earnestly, like his father. Pam nodded her head in the bright red tam. Susan wondered what they were saying, but she was so relieved to see them, she forget to question them about it.

"Did you have any trouble today?"

"No," said Pam.

"Not much," said Harvey.

"Well, did they try to fight? Did they just let you alone?"

"We—talked," said Pam evasively. "We—talked to people. Coral Emmert is a friend of a boy, and she said she'd talk to him."

Susan was puzzled. "What boy? Was he one of the gang?"

"No, he has another gang. He's Fred Goss."

"Oh. Well, can he stop them from attacking you?"

"I guess so, if it works out. But don't talk about it, Mom. That might spoil it."

"Oh," said Susan blankly. Pam went to do her homework.

Harvey added, "You let us work it out, Mom. I think we can. You just have to have an angle."

"An angle. You mean friends? And being in a gang?"

"Yep. We'll work it out. Got anything to eat?"

She was sidetracked into satisfying his voracious appetite. But she worried about Harvey, and even more about Pam, working silently in her room. Her radio wasn't on, nor was her record player going. Pam had always loved music...

After supper, she suggested, "Would you like to hear the new records I got in Franklin? You haven't heard them all."

To her surprise, they refused.

"No, Mom, a fellow's coming over. I'm going to help him with his reading," said Harvey. "The gang wants me to."

"Oh." She surveyed him in surprise. But he seemed to think it was the thing to do, and it did not seem to be anything to worry about. "What about you, Pam?"

"I want to practice something."

"Something" turned out to be makeup. Pam had bought powder, rouge and lipstick. "Coral said the powder would cover the bruises."

"Yes, I guess it will," Susan agreed soberly.

She went back to the kitchen, and spent the evening there, worrying about the children. Harvey was getting involved in a gang. Pam was trying to conform to the dubious standards of the girls of New Harmony.

Maybe this would save them from being beaten up. But did the right solution lie in joining a gang? "If you can't lick them, join them?"

But Susan saw only trouble ahead. And she could not see any way of avoiding it. She had tried—and failed.

For years she had weakly depended on Paul for everything. She had never tried to stand alone. Now Paul had withdrawn his support. She was trying to stand, and hold up Pam and Harvey too. And it did not work.

She was a weakling, a futile, desperate woman with no real strength. Staring out at the dark fields behind the house, she saw clearly why she was failing her children. She had never tried to be strong and sure. Now when she needed strength, she had none.

True strength did not grow overnight. It had to be built slowly, carefully. She had never needed it before. It had seemed more important for her as a woman to learn music, art, the gentler interests of life. She had never thought she would have to know how to fight.

CHAPTER EIGHT

PAUL did not come home Tuesday night. He telephoned on Wednesday and said he would not be home that evening either.

"How is Pam?" he asked as an afterthought.

"She's wearing heavy makeup over the bruises so they won't show. Harvey is joining a gang so he won't get beaten up," Susan told him. He did not seem to understand her heavy sarcasm.

"Fine," he said heartily.

"Paul, it isn't right!" she burst out. "This isn't the right answer! They don't belong here. They—"

He hung up. She heard the hard click in her ear, and then silence.

Duane was shaking the smaller rugs and hanging them on the line. When he came back into the house, she burst out at him. "Paul won't even listen to me! He hung up!"

"He doesn't understand," said Duane mildly. "Wait a while. See how things work out. Maybe they'll get along all right."

She shook her head, her mouth pressed tight. "They'll learn to adjust. They're intelligent. They'll learn to get along, to do what the others do. But the cost! I dread what they'll have to give up. Now they are individuals, learning to think for themselves, discovering music, art, books. These people laughed at things like that—a person likes good music, they call him a sissy."

"Yes, I know. It's because they're not used to it. They don't hear any good music—just rock and roll. So they think anybody that likes it must be crazy."

"How can I teach my children about good music, then? How can I help them understand art and plays, if they never see any—if all their friends laugh at them? Oh, Duane, my children will live here, but they'll be as stunted as trees in a harsh wind. They'll use all their energies in a fight for existence, for conformity. They'll have no strength left to be individuals—to know and love good things."

Duane had no answer for her. His troubled green eyes watched her as she moved around the kitchen.

"I wish I could help," he said wistfully.

"Oh, you do help, you do!" She turned to him, and put her hands to his face, caressing his thin young cheeks. "I don't know what I'd do without you. You help me with all this heavy work—"

"Oh, I don't do much." He flushed at the praise, his hands holding her arms.

"This big house is so different from the apartment. You're so good to me, with all the work you do. But more than that, you care what happens to me. And you listen to me blowing up."

"You have to talk to somebody." His hands had gone to her waist, caressingly.

"And you listen." She drew his head down to kiss his lips. She was always surprised at the hard maturity of his mouth. He seemed such a boy, but his caresses were not boyish. Her mouth opened under the insistence of his. Her head fell back against his arm. She felt suddenly weak and helpless in his strong grasp. The pressure of his body against hers aroused her hungers, and she clung to him.

"Let's go to your room now," he whispered after a few moments. Desire had risen as swiftly in him as in her and she could feel the urgency of his touch.

"Yes. Yes, I want—" He kissed her lingeringly, his mouth fiery hot now. They went to her room.

He undressed swiftly, then sat on the edge of the bed to watch her. Sometimes she was embarrassed by his frank interest, and turned from his gaze, keeping her back to him.

When she was ready she went over to him. She felt his gaze caress her and a new gentle heat stole over her. His earnest, adoring eyes not only told her that he thought her beautiful—they made her feel so.

"Oh, you're so pretty, you're so pretty," he said. He drew her down and kissed her, his hands on the softness of her waist. She held his head against her, and ran her fingers through the tight blond curls. She liked it when he nuzzled against her this way. She liked the tight grasp of his strong arms around her. She felt safe and warm and secure, and she could push the world away for a while.

She was so grateful to him. If Duane had not been around to help and sustain her, what would have happened to her?

Partly from gratitude because she, too, had found a new richness in their relationship, partly from genuine desire, she fell against him, teaching him caresses he had not known before. She led him on slowly, finding a deep satisfaction in feeling his wonderment vanish, masculine certainty taking its place. Even if she had to hurt him later, at least he would grow into a fuller man than Paul—he would understand a woman's side of love.

As he drew her closer, she felt the heavy thumping of his heart. In moments, they were tightly together.

She discovered her pleasure in his increasingly competent ardor.

He laughed in mannish ecstacy and hugged her. They sat together silently for a while, enjoying a new intimacy. His hands caressed her breasts, her waist and thighs, moving slowly over her.

Finally she stirred, and stood up slowly. She lay down on the bed, and he clasped her afresh and lay above her, watching her face as he finished the embrace hungrily.

"I like it best this way, seeing you at the same time," he said huskily. "You're so beautiful. Everything you are is beautiful. You're the most beautiful thing in the world."

She drew him down closer to her and held him tightly in her arms, moved beyond words.

Later, she put on a negligee and went downstairs. She put several records on the player, then went back upstairs to him.

He smiled at her when she came into the room, a radiant smile of pleasure.

"Music," he said.

"Yes. I like to hear it—always." She lay down beside him again.

This time while they made love to each other, the music poured through the house. They were surrounded by sound; they swam in melody, drowned in rapturous harmonies. Their desires were roused more keenly, they drew out their embraces to greater lengths, moving in cadence like dancing.

Susan beat out the melody of one rhythm on Duane's back as they lay together, her fingers drumming lightly on him. He smiled at her, bending to touch her breasts with his lips, lightly, possessively.

She had not felt like this with Paul, in all their married life. That thought kept recurring to her, like a discordant note in the harmony of their movements. Never, never had she given to Paul what she gave gladly, liberally, to this boy. Paul liked music, enjoyed the concerts they had attended, studied the lives of composers, and talked learnedly of etudes and concertos. Yet it never would have occurred to him to make music a stimulus and an integral part of their passion.

The music was building to a climax. Duane and she drowned in floods of music and ecstacy together.

In the next few hours they learned much more as the music flowed on around them. The music had broken through what reticence they still felt with each other.

Susan told him things she had never told anyone, even Paul, things about her dreams as a girl, her disappointments, her friends, her joys, her hopes. "I wanted to create beauty, somehow.

Yet I felt I didn't have the talent for painting, or writing, or playing the piano. I studied the piano for years, but my hands aren't big enough, or my talent."

He kissed her hands.

"Big enough for this," he teased gently. "And you've created something—what about your two children?"

"Thank you for saying that," she said. She kissed him. "I like photography. There I feel I can accomplish something. I can see pictures. I can't draw them, but I can take them on film."

She told him about her first sales to a magazine, how thrilled and excited she had been. "I bought four copies. Paul laughed. He said it would cost me more in film and copies of the magazine and I'd ever get in payment."

"But it wasn't the pay," said Duane. "It was making something."

"Yes. To create—to find beauty—Sometimes I think the world is so ugly and confused that the only purpose worth while is to find beauty in it. If you can't find any beauty, you might as well die."

"You'll find it. You know where to look," said Duane. He drew her up so that her slim body was curled warmly in the bend of his body. "You know so much. If only I could know—"

"You will. But Duane, you ought to leave here. You ought to go to college. You won't get anywhere clerking in the store. You should go to college."

"I can't afford it."

She thought for a little. "If you would move to a town where there was a college, you could afford it. You could work part-time and go to college part-time. Lots of kids do. They work their way through. It takes longer, but when they graduate, they can get much better jobs at higher pay. And Duane, you'll have time for music, and art. You'll learn about important things. Oh, I envy you—you're free. You can go where you please. If only I could go back and finish college—"

She sighed. No. There was no going back for her. She could only stumble forward.

"I don't know what I'd study," said Duane thoughtfully. "I don't know what I could do. What do you think I could?"

"What did you like in school?"

"Oh—lots of things. Arithmetic, reading, science. What does that add up to?"

"Teaching," she said promptly. "Duane, you'd be a good teacher. You're very good and patient with children."

"Oh, gee, I couldn't do that!"

"Yes, you could. But you'd have to go to college first."

The music stopped. The records were finished. She looked at the bedside clock. "Two-thirty. Oh, I'd better get up." She gave him a quick kiss.

"Just a minute." He rolled over to her, bent down, and kissed her long, deeply. She sighed as he lifted up again.

"Oh, it was good—good, today."

"It was beautiful." He watched her get up, then he finally got out of bed himself, and dressed.

He stayed and helped her finish cleaning the living room and dining room. By that time, the children had come home from school.

Pamela brought a friend, Coral Emmert. Susan could scarcely keep from staring at her the whole time. This girl, a friend of Pam's?

Coral was fourteen, two years older than Pam. She wore heavy makeup that would have been startling on a woman of twenty-five. Her eyebrows were plucked to a thin line, her lipstick thick. She wore a tan foundation and powder that looked caked in the sunlight. Her green eyeshadow gave her eyes a weird cast. But worst of all was the hair, naturally a light brown, streaked with inexpertly applied silver-blonde dye.

Pam took her mother out to the kitchen to help her fix gingerale.

"Pam, that girl—" Susan began.

"I know! But Mom, be nice to her! It's terribly important."

"Pam, her clothes—" Coral's skirt was too short and too tight. When she sat down, one could see halfway up her plump thighs. Her sweater, of a brilliant red, was a size too small, and strained her full breasts. "They're too tight. And do all the girls wear hose and high-heeled shoes to grade school?"

"The popular ones do, Mom. And she thinks I should too. Please, Mom! I've got to!"

Susan gazed into the desperate blue eyes, the anxious face of her young daughter. "We'll—see," she said, turning away.

"Mom, it's important. Could I wear my red dress and my patent leather heels tomorrow? And can I buy some new heels? I need some suede heels, Coral says."

Coral came out to the kitchen. "I been telling Pam she's a real cute doll, Mrs. Lambert," she said, chewing gum vigorously. "She needs fixing up, though. You leave her to me, and she'll be the most popular girl in seventh grade."

"It's very kind of you, I'm sure," Susan began slowly. Pam gave her a quick frantic look. "Very kind," said Susan, trying to make her voice warm and friendly.

"She'll need a new dress for the dance, too. Good thing she's got a date. Now, I thought a black dress would be good. Get her noticed!"

"Black!" gasped Susan. "Oh, no! She's too young for black. I think a pink—"

"Oh, no, not pink," said Coral. "That's too babyish."

"We'll—go shopping soon," said Susan. "But, Pam, I don't think it should be black. What about rose, or blue—"

"Blue might be nice," said Coral. " 'Cause she's got blue eyes. Yeah, I think blue would be okay."

Pam looked as relieved and awed as though Coral had made a major fashion decree. "Oh, that's good. Isn't that good, Mom? I could wear blue, Coral says."

Susan talked about it to Duane the next morning. "'Coral says' is going to be a popular phrase around here, I can see that," she sighed. "But oh, Duane, we've got to move away fast. That girl is just about the worst friend Pam could ever have. I guess she's useful enough in protecting her from being beaten up, but I can't take very much of her!"

"She's tough, all right," said Duane. "What are your chances of moving? Is he willing to move soon?"

"He can't see the need, not yet. But if he could just see Coral and Pam together, that might do it."

Lying in Duane's arms, trying to lose herself in the pleasure of his love, she went on worrying about Pam's new friendship. Her baby daughter, her lovely, gentle girl. What would become of her? How long could she be a friend of a girl like Coral Emmert without being damaged beyond repair?

The formal. It ought to be very simple, very plain, a pretty pastel blue. Would Pam be satisfied with that? More important, would Coral be satisfied?

How sophisticated was Coral, anyway? She wouldn't be as bad as she looked. She was only fourteen. She was probably just imitating some older girls. And maybe she kissed boys, and was considered daring. But no more than that—no more—not at fourteen.

"What are you thinking about?" asked Duane.

She sighed, and turned toward him. "I don't want to think any more. Help me not to think."

He drew her up to sit in his lap on the bed. "All right," he said, laughing a little. "We won't think any more!"

"What are you doing? Duane!" He pulled her up on his knees, drew her to him. She felt the sudden shock of his forcefulness. She clasped her arms around his neck.

"Wait—" she gasped, but he would not.

He made love to her swiftly, expertly. All thoughts and all worries blurred from her mind. She could not think of anything but his newly found manhood, his sureness, his certainty of her reactions to his, the feel of his body against hers.

He was in control the rest of the day, as a man ought to be in control, yet for all his growing assertiveness, his love never violated some inmost place in her spirit. He did not make her feel, as Paul did, like something a man used, a bought body. Marriage—the man-woman contract—ought always to be like this. Even in violence, kindness ... without words, understanding.

Duane had been ready for his first affair. Better this for him, she thought, not looking ahead for herself but only for him, than a frightened dangerous coupling with a girl his own age, a girl like Coral ... and the trouble that came after, when children, without guidance, played early grown-up games. The sweetness of this moment ...

Already he seemed more like her husband than Paul did. She had confided to Duane her inmost thoughts, her concerns, her worries.

And he had understood.

And in love, his understanding of her needs was far more keen than Paul's had ever been. He seemed to know from the first her need for caresses, for kisses. He could arouse her, make her respond, bring her to fulfillment over and over as her husband had rarely done.

She was already aware that her husband had not known her truly. Now she was beginning to realize that she had scarcely known herself, or her possibilities. This boy was showing her the image of herself as she really was, a woman capable of deep, rich passion and ecstasy.

CHAPTER NINE

SUSAN had made a resolution for herself. She could not force Duane to keep it. He came over on Thursday morning.

"I've got the morning to kill," he said. "What can I do for you today?"

Only one thought came to her mind, and she blushed. Paul had not come home again last night. She found it terribly difficult to maintain her anger with him over his affair, because she was having one herself. It was confusing.

"Why don't you rest?" she suggested, trying not to think of the bed. "You work so hard all week."

"Good idea." He grinned, looking like a mischievous child. "Come with me." It was the first time he had proposed to her.

"Oh, Duane, I—I shouldn't—"

"Don't you want to?" But he was not crushed and hurt. He looked at her as though he knew just what she was thinking.

"You know—I do—but—"

She was just beginning to explain, when he pulled her to him and started kissing her. They went to bed.

It was two hours later when she remembered her resolution. She tried to explain to him that they must not make love any more.

He listened gravely. It was a little ridiculous, because they were lying naked beside each other, and the only reason he was not kissing her was because he had just finished making love to her for the fifth time, and they were both a little tired.

"Then the only reason you think we shouldn't make love is so I won't be hurt?"

"Not the only reason. But it's the main one."

"So I have a choice. I can make love to you now, and be hurt later when it has to end. Or I can be hurt now—by not being allowed to kiss you any more. I choose love now."

He bent over her and kissed her into silence. Sometimes he did not seem like a boy any more, for all his lean youthfulness, his awkward movements, his frank curiosity. He was a man in the way he caressed her, drew her, fired her passion, and then brought them together in a final embrace of complete ecstasy.

It was a frightening experience in a way. Susan had never felt such emotions as she felt today, not even with Paul in their early days of marriage.

Duane left for work soon after two o'clock. After he left, Susan got up and dressed again. She seemed to do a great deal of dressing and undressing these days, she thought in amusement. Yet she felt more light-hearted after Duane had been with her. She could not sink down into depression, after having been so high in ecstasy, her body so aroused and so satisfied.

The mail came about two-thirty. She leafed through it idly. It was mostly ads. Then she saw the letter, long white business envelope with the return address of *Field and City Street,* the magazine to which she had just sent the photographs of the ugly fields and town of New Harmony. Could they be buying her pictures, so soon?

She sat down and ripped open the envelope.

"Mrs. Paul Wladek" and the address in Franklin were at the top of the letter. She glanced at the envelope again. Yes, it had been forwarded from the apartment.

Dear Mrs. Wladek:

It has been some time since we've received any photos from you. We have always appreciated your interest in our magazine, and hope to hear from you again soon with more of your excellent pix.

How nice of them, she thought, leaning back and reading the first paragraph again. How nice to know her work was liked so much that they had bothered to write to her!

However, we are not writing just about your photos. It so happens that one of our editors is leaving within two months, and there will be an opening on our staff. Have you ever considered working for a magazine? May we ask also if you have had any editorial experience?

As you live in Franklin, and the quality of your work has attracted our attention, we are interested in seeing you about this position. We do not know your situation, and you may not be interested in working.

We will be glad to hear from you, though, and will be glad to have you drop in to talk this over. And even if you don't care about the job, we'll be glad to see more of your pix, as always.

Sincerely,
Victor Crandall,
Editor
Field and City Street

"For goodness sake," Susan breathed aloud, staring at the letter. How wonderful of them! How nice of them! They liked her work so well, they seriously considered her as an editor! How fabulous! How amazing!

She got up and danced around the room, holding the letter before her delightedly. She stopped to read it again. "The quality of your work—"

"Oh, my," she said. "Oh, my goodness. Oh-oh-oh!"

Oh, for somebody to tell about this! But Duane had left. The children were in school. She thought of calling Jill Ohms. No. Jill would say, "But you're not thinking of getting a job, are you? Paul wouldn't approve!"

Paul wouldn't approve.

Susan sobered. She sat down on the couch again and thought, long and hard. A job. An editorial job. It would pay pretty well, probably. Better than a secretarial job, better than a clerk. Enough to support herself, and Pam and Harvey.

She could move back to Franklin. She would have to live in Franklin. She would not commute as Paul did. Besides, she vaguely remembered that the magazine's offices were open on Saturday morning. She had taken some rush photos up to a secretary one Saturday morning. She had had the impression of a controlled confusion, a quiet rushing of workers, of many desks, books, papers.

She closed her eyes, trying to remember. They had two floors of a building. The editorial offices were in the front of one floor, overlooking the river. The walls were pale green, the carpets reddish brown, the drapes a golden brown. Quiet, thoughtful people, several men wearing horn-rimmed glasses, several secretaries typing.

"An editor! Me!" It was probably an assistant editor's job. Editorial experience? She read the letter again. She did not have any experience, except with photographs. Oh, yes, she wrote her own captions, and sometimes she had written long paragraphs of descriptions. Was that editorial experience?

Were they *seriously* considering her? Oh, for someone to talk to!

She looked at the date of the letter. Last Saturday! She groaned. It had taken several days for the letter to be forwarded. Oh, the job might be filled. She ought to write—or phone—

But did she want the job? Paul would be furious. He was very emphatic in his views about married women working, especially women with children—most especially Susan.

Her mouth tightened. If she took the job—even if Paul left them—she could move back to Franklin, take the children with her, put them back in school there, give them the cultural advantages that had been snatched so rudely from them.

It wouldn't hurt to find out about the job. She could talk to the editor, Mr. Crandall.

There was a telephone number on the letterhead. She went to the phone and dialed the long distance operator. "I wish to call Franklin 9-7600."

"Thank you." A pause.

"Temple Publications."

"Good afternoon. May I speak to Mr. Victor Crandall, please?"

"May I ask who's calling?"

"Mrs. Susan Wladek."

"Thank you."

She heard the click of the phones, then a man's voice said, "Vic Crandall."

"Mr. Crandall? This is Mrs. Susan Wladek."

The man's voice warmed from business-like briskness to cordiality. "Well, Mrs. Wladek! I'm happy to hear from you. We just got some pix from you this morning from New Harmony."

"Yes. We moved. But it isn't very satisfactory," she said steadily. Her hands were shaking.

"I hope you're interested in our proposition."

"Yes, I am. I'd like to talk to you about it."

"Good. When can you come over?"

"Would Saturday morning be all right?"

"Fine. Shall we say about nine-thirty?"

"Yes. That's fine. Nine-thirty."

"Good. We'll be expecting you."

"Mr. Crandall—one thing more. I—I don't have editorial experience. At least, I've never worked on a magazine before."

"That may be more of a help than a hindrance!" said the man's warm voice. "We'll teach you our methods, then! Now, don't worry. We like your new pix too. Terrific job. I'll talk to you about them Saturday."

"Thank you. Yes. Goodbye." She hung up, shaking like a leaf, and smiling at nothing. They liked her pictures. They liked her work. They wanted to talk to her. It did not matter about her lack of editorial experience.

She laughed shakily, out loud. This was her chance. She must go in on Saturday.

But she must not tell anyone why. She bit her fingernail nervously. What reason could she give for going in to town on Saturday? She would have to get the seven-thirty bus to get to her appointment by nine-thirty. What reason for all this hurry?

Pam's dress—the blue formal. Yes, and errands. Many errands. She would not let Pam go along. She must not know yet.

Susan decided not to tell anyone, except perhaps Duane—not till it was definite. They might change their minds, even that nice Mr. Crandall who thought her photos were "terrific."

She sang happily at her work that afternoon. Oh, things could not go on being bad indefinitely. She would, she would rescue the children from this horrible place, even at the cost of losing Paul.

Losing Paul … She sobered suddenly. She had not really, seriously considered losing Paul. He was a very proud man. He had said many times it was a humiliation for any man's wife to get a job—it said quite plainly that she did not trust her husband to support her.

Yet she did not want to lose Paul. He was her husband. They had been married thirteen years. She had adored him—she still loved him, in spite of his exasperating ways this summer. Olivia Belgrove was to blame for that. Once he was cured of his infatuation for her, he and Susan could be happy again.

Susan did not want a divorce. She could not imagine being divorced from Paul. This summer, seeing him only infrequently, being estranged from him, quarreling so much, had been a torment to her. She wanted them to be happy again, to be together again, going to concerts, planning for the children, sleeping together.

Oh, it was all such a mess! If only they had never left Franklin! She did not want to do things that would make him unhappy. This job would enrage him. Yet—yet, if it was the only way to get the children out of New Harmony, back to Franklin, she must take it, no matter what Paul thought or did.

Paul came home late again Thursday night. She wondered if his lateness and tiredness were due to over-work, or over-Olivia? She bit her tongue until it was sore, to keep from asking him about Olivia, and from telling him about the job offer.

He saw Pam wearing heavy makeup—and said not a word. He saw the bruises on Harvey's face—and said nothing. That angered her deeply, and steeled her resolution to go ahead to find out about the job.

"I'm going into Franklin Saturday," she told him casually, about nine o'clock. "I want to get a formal for Pam's dance next Saturday. And I have loads of other errands."

Paul frowned. "You'll have to get someone to stay with the children. I'm staying in town this weekend."

"Oh, Paul, not again!" She stared at him in dismay. "I have to go in Saturday, and there's nobody to stay with the children."

"Take them along, then. And find a baby sitter! You don't have to make things so hard for everyone, Susan! You manufacture difficulties all the time. It is not like you."

"I'm not like myself," she said ironically, thinking of how she was with Duane. "I've changed. You'll hardly know me any more."

He frowned at her. The children were listening, wide-eyed and uncertain.

"Well, work it out. I can't always change my plans to suit you."

She bit her lip to hold back a sharp rejoinder. The rest of the evening, she worried about what to do on Saturday. Was there any woman she knew in New Harmony with whom she could trust the children? No, no one.

She could not take them along. She could just see the children waiting in the lounge at Temple Publications while their mother applied for a job. Mr. Crandall might well ask her why she didn't stay home to look after them.

Maybe she could bring them in to Franklin, and leave them with Jill Ohms. For a moment she considered it seriously. No. She must not involve Jill, and she did not want others to know about it yet.

As usual, she turned to Duane with her problem. She showed him the letter. He was very impressed.

"My gosh! Susan, that is terrific! An editor! Golly!"

His delight was balm to her troubled spirit. "I was thrilled. Imagine their asking me!"

"Gee, they must really like your pictures! Golly, that is terrific. Super!"

For a few minutes she allowed herself to rejoice in his excitement. Then she remembered the obstacles.

"I made an appointment to see Mr. Crandall Saturday morning. Only now Paul says he won't be home this weekend, and I can't just leave the children."

"There's nobody to leave them with," said Duane. "Yeah—I guess—" He seemed to be thinking deeply, his excitement fading. "Gee, Susan, what about the kids? When you're working, I mean?"

"I haven't figured it all out," she admitted frankly. "I know this much—we'll move back to Franklin. We must. That's the main reason I'm considering this job. If I—I have the sole care of the children, I think I'll get an apartment at a place I know. There's an older woman who runs the apartment house. I've known her for years. I could leave the children with her until I get home from work."

"You mean, your husband might leave you?"

"Yes. He might. He never wanted me to work. And he is very stubborn about staying in New Harmony."

"I see." Duane was silent for a while.

She folded and refolded the letter nervously. They were sitting on the couch in the living room.

Duane said finally, "I knew something was awfully wrong for you. I guess I don't know what to tell you. You know better than I do what you want. But I'll help all I can. I'll take Saturday off and stay with the kids. That's the least I can do."

"You will? Oh, Duane, you shouldn't. Saturday is such a big day at the store, and they're awful about letting you off."

He shrugged. "I just might not stay, very much longer. Maybe I'll take your advice and move away. Go to college somewhere."

"Oh, you should—you ought to."

"Well, that's later. For now, you go in to Franklin tomorrow. Take your time about seeing about the job, and Pam's formal, and all that. I'll be here all day."

"Thank you." She kissed him, and he smiled with pleasure. One thing led to another, and they were soon in bed together. Maybe it was sort of bribery, Susan thought, much later, but she got every bit as much pleasure from it as Duane seemed to.

While they were resting, she thought again of the letter and her phone conversation with Mr. Crandall.

"Oh, Duane, isn't it wonderful?"

"This?" He touched her.

"Yes. But also the job. They liked my pictures."

He chuckled. "Is that what you've been thinking about while I was working away so hard?"

"Oh, silly! No. When you make love to me I can't think of anything else. It's just that I'm so happy; everything seemed so bad, except for you. You were the only good thing that I've had since we moved here."

"You're the only good thing I've ever had."

She turned to him. "I'll miss you," she whispered passionately. "I'll hate leaving you. It'll hurt—"

"Me, too. But at least—we've had this much. I'll never forget you."

They kissed, slowly.

"Besides," he added. "you haven't left yet. We have more time."

"Yes. More. More. And I want more. Lots more time—with you—"

CHAPTER TEN

SUSAN had a lot of time to think during the long bus ride into the city Saturday morning. It was early enough for the bus not to be crowded, and she had the double seat to herself.

The first incredulous delight had faded somewhat. She wanted the job, yes. But Pam and Harvey were young. They needed her. Working during the week while they were in school would not be so bad, but working on Saturday was another matter.

And Paul— She must not accept any job, no matter how promising, before discussing it with Paul. This was not a decision to be made lightly, or in time of anger at her husband. She did not want to break up her marriage.

She wondered how serious he was about Olivia. Was he thinking of divorce? He had kept up the affair much longer than she had thought he would. Looking back, she realized he must have been having an affair with Olivia since May, at least. And this was the middle of October.

He was staying in town this weekend. For business, or Olivia? She decided she might just as well check on that also. She would call the office after her interview with Mr. Crandall. If Miss Finch put her off with vague answers, she would go out to Olivia's house.

The idea made her tremble; she hated scenes. The fact of spying on Paul was bad enough. Should she confront them? If she did, would it automatically break up their marriage? Paul always got so furiously angry at her when she tried to tell him he was wrong. Would he blow up and leave them, if she made a scene about his affair?

Another thought occurred to her. Maybe she was not being fair to Paul. She was taking the word of other people that he and Olivia were intimate. He might not be involved with her at all. He might have a great deal of work that was keeping him busy. And the work might be Olivia's. After all, her husband had been a customer of Paul's...

Susan was tired and warm after the long ride, and the smell of the exhaust fumes of the bus clung to her clothes. She went to the rest room of a department store, shook out her suit jacket, put on fresh powder and lipstick, and combed her hair.

She had meant to arrive early for the appointment, but the delay caused her to arrive a minute late. However, the girl at the reception desk told her that Mr. Crandall would be busy for a few minutes, and offered her a chair.

Susan was glad enough to sit down and catch her breath, and calm herself. She looked about the large open offices. There was the same controlled confusion she had remembered. Typewriters were clicking rapidly; a boy dashed in with some large brown envelopes and several pages of galley proofs, and distributed them at three different desks.

The desks were large. Each had a huge lighted desk lamp, stacks of papers, a telephone. The numbers of men and women were about equal, she estimated. Most wore glasses. She wondered if she would need glasses after working here for a while.

The women wore suits or dark cotton dresses. Most wore shoes that looked sensible—medium-height heels. Hats? She saw some coat racks, and there were a goodly number of women's hats on them—conservative, business-like hats.

"Mr. Crandall is ready now," said the receptionist. She took Susan back to a desk in the far corner.

"This is Mr. Crandall, Mrs. Wladek," the girl said, and departed.

Mr. Crandall stood up, smiled and shook her hand. "Sorry to have kept you waiting, Mrs. Wladek."

"That's quite all right." She seated herself in the chair beside his desk.

He sat down in his swivel chair, and switched off the large desk lamp. "Easier on the eyes," he explained.

She thought he was in his early forties. He was getting bald, his dark hair receding from his forehead at the temples. His dark eyes were sharp and keen behind the black horn-rimmed glasses. She liked the crinkles around his eyes, and he had a quick smile. In just a few minutes, she decided he would be nice to work for.

"You said you hadn't had any editorial experience, Mrs. Wladek."

"No, none."

"Any college?"

"Two years." She told him her educational experience. "I worked as a secretary to pay my way. Then my fiancé started his own importing business, and we decided to get married."

"He's an importer, then?"

"Yes." She told him about Paul's firm. "We have two children, a girl of twelve and a boy of nine."

"Who are gradually growing up, and leaving you with less to do?"

"Yes, in a way." She answered his smile. "Actually, the house in New Harmony is so big and overwhelming, it keeps me busy doing housework."

"Ah." He leaned back in the chair. "How long a ride is it to commute?"

"Much too long. If I do take a job, I plan to move back to Franklin. I'm not satisfied with the community there. I want more cultural advantages for the children, as well as for my husband and myself."

"I see. That's very interesting. You know, we almost bought a house in the suburbs a couple years ago. It was an hour each way. Cute house, lots of grass, all that. Then I thought, two hours out of every day? Nothing doing. I'd rather spend that time with the kids in a city park than let them play alone on a grassy lawn. I'm the selfish type."

"I don't think so at all!" she said vehemently. "One of the worst parts of living so far out is the fact we seldom see my husband. When he has extra work in the evenings, he stays at a friend's apartment rather than ride back and forth. And I understand the roads are quite bad in winter."

He nodded. She realized that his friendliness and interest had drawn her out of her reticence, and had caused her to tell him more than she meant to about herself and her family.

"Well, I expect you'd like to know first what we do here," he said cheerfully. "I'll show you around, introduce you to our staff, and explain how our magazine gets printed each month."

The next hour was an interesting one for Susan. Victor Crandall (everyone called him "Vic") introduced her to each staff member in turn, and each explained briefly what his job was. Susan looked at layouts for the next issues, at dummies, galleys, page proofs, illustrations. She visited the darkrooms, business offices, circulation department, mailing department.

"We don't print here," Vic explained. "That's done by a commercial printer. They send proofs back here to us. Bud, here, is just back with some." He indicated the messenger boy dashing across the office.

He had arranged the tour so they ended up at his desk again. They sat down.

"Have I worn you out?" he asked, smiling.

"Oh, no! It's been very interesting."

"Well, what do you think? Are you interested in the job?"

"I want it," she said simply.

"Good!"

"But I—I'll have to have some time. I must tell my husband about it, and make sure it's all right. The Saturday work is a problem."

"Yes, it has been for all of us. Starting January first, we're going to cut out the Saturday work, and see what happens. We may have to work a little longer, or do some writing or proofreading at home, but we all feel we want to give it a try."

"Oh, that's wonderful! I don't want to be away when the children are home all day. Summers, they will probably go to camp, so there'll only be a couple of weeks when I'll need a woman to look after them."

They talked a while longer, and Susan told him she would let him know within a couple of weeks if she could take the job. "It will mean moving back to Franklin, and I'm not sure yet just when we can do that," she told him frankly. "If you find someone else who suits you better, I won't blame you for hiring him."

He smiled. "No. I think you're the right one for this job. You know, it was that last set of pix that really convinced me."

"The ugly ones?"

"Yes. A lot of people can photograph beauty and make it appealing. But it takes a real artist to find design and purpose in the ugly."

He accompanied her to the door, and was very kind and cordial. She promised to let him know as soon as possible, and went away in a daze. She walked down the street staring ahead, scarcely knowing where she was going. She woke and laughed to herself when she found herself in front of the Music Hall, looking at the posters for the next concert.

No, she probably would not be able to go to the next concert. But soon—soon—she would be back in Franklin, able to go to concerts and art galleries and good stores once more.

Stores! Pam's formal!

She had forgotten it entirely. She turned and hurried back toward the nearest department store.

It took her a long time to choose something suitable for Pam that would be considered glamorous enough by Coral. She settled on a vivid blue formal, with a discreet jacket covering a modestly cut neckline. Then she found a strand of iridescent crystal beads, and some tiny sparkling earrings to match. She completed the outfit with a blue velvet bag and a small blue compact.

Tired but satisfied, she sat down in a restaurant for a quick lunch and a cup of coffee. The formal would be delivered on Monday. Surely Pam would like it. The business of choosing the dress and accessories had brought her down from the cloud where the interview had send her.

Paul. Now she must consider Paul. She wanted to find out for herself if he were really having an affair with Olivia.

She had a second cup of coffee while she pondered what she would do.

After lunch, she found a telephone in a quiet spot in the department store. First she called the office. Miss Finch answered.

"Is Mr. Paul Wladek there?" she asked bruskly, hoping the secretary would not recognize her voice.

"No, ma'am, he won't be in today."

"Oh. Thank you."

"May I take a message for him?"

"No, thank you. I'll call him Monday."

She hung up, then phoned the apartment of the friend with whom Paul stayed overnight in town. The phone rang and rang. No one answered.

That was that. There was no way of checking now, unless she went out to Olivia's house, or phoned there. She frowned. No, she would not phone. They would only deny that Paul was there—if he was.

Finally she took a bus out to Olivia Belgrove's house. It was in an exclusive neighborhood, with parks, huge lawns, enormous houses. There was a park opposite the Belgrove house, and benches under the trees. She walked toward the park. It was a warm day, and she felt hot from rushing around. She found a bench in the shade, from which she could see the house.

She sat down, and composed herself. Then she glanced over toward the house, as though casually interested in seeing the homes of the neighborhood.

The first thing she noticed was Paul's car in the driveway, under the portico.

She was abruptly, furiously angry. So there he was, in that house! He had forced them to move to the drab, dangerous suburbs, so he could play around in undiscovered bliss with a divorced blonde.

She waited grimly for several hours. Paul might come out. She would wait till dusk and see. She was more tired than she had realized. She had been up since before six that morning. The long bus ride, with the stifling exhaust fumes and the heat, had been wearying. The excitement of the interview had buoyed her up for a while. Then the tiring search for just the right formal, a lovely necklace, the bag to match, had worn her out further.

She sat for a long time in the park, watching the squirrels playing in the leaves and bushes, looking at the birds darting about the trees. There were several cardinals, their bright red bodies flickering against the green.

Soon the leaves would be turning red, brown and yellow as the frost bit them and the wind snatched them from the branches. Usually she liked autumn. It was the time of beginnings for her: school started once more, the concert season began, the art galleries put on new shows, the theater season began again. She had always liked fall clothes best—the smart plaid woolens, rich ruby velvets, the glowing silk jerseys and lustrous fur jackets.

Perhaps she was getting too tired and stale. Perhaps it was the overshadowing pall of the prospect of a winter in New Harmony. What if nothing happened—what if she failed, and they had to remain in that dreadful place? She shivered, even in the warm air of the park.

It was almost five o'clock when she saw the house door opening. Paul came out. Behind him, Susan could make out the form of a woman dressed in something black and filmy.

Susan watched in cold rage as they exchanged a long kiss. Then Paul went over to the car and got in.

Susan had never been clever in her dealings with people. She had been amazed at Paul, at how he could manipulate people, at how he could twist their words and tangle them in nets they never knew they were weaving. Now she would have to pit herself against this clever man, her husband, and use the knowledge of his affair as a wedge to get them out of New Harmony and back to Franklin.

How could she do all this without losing him in the process? She was not hard and tough. She could not get along in this world very well alone. She needed him, she wanted him. Life would be poorer for her without him. Yet—and yet—

By the time the bus arrived at the station in New Harmony, it was dark outside. Susan took a taxi home. Her head ached, her body ached, she was tired and cross and afraid.

PART 2

CHAPTER ELEVEN

THE first thing Susan saw, after she paid the taxi driver and turned toward the house, was Paul's car in the driveway.

She was close to fainting with the shock. Her knees trembled and she could scarcely walk to the front door. Could she have been mistaken? Had it been another car at Olivia's door? No, of course not. Paul had come out and had driven away.

Paul met her at the door. "Susan! We were beginning to get worried about you."

"I'm late," she said vaguely.

Paul took her jacket and hat, her bag and gloves. "You poor darling, you look completely worn out."

Pam came from the kitchen. "Oh, Mummy, we were getting scared."

"Pam got dinner," said Paul proudly. "She is a good cook."

"That's fine. Where's Harvey?"

"He went out with some friends," said Pam. "He said he'd be home by dark."

"It's dark now." Susan peered out the window anxiously.

"Now, don't baby the boy! He is growing up," said Paul.

"Mummy, did you get my formal?" Pam asked. "Did you find one for me?"

Susan smiled at her. "Oh, yes, I did. A lovely blue one."

"Not a baby blue?"

"No, not a baby blue. It's a bright vivid blue. They're sending it out Monday."

"Oh." Pam didn't look much happier. "I'll ask Coral to come home with me after school and make sure it looks all right."

Paul raised his eyebrows at Susan, and his eyes sparkled with amusement. Susan did not feel amused.

"Have you had dinner, Mummy?" asked Pam. "I'm just starting the dishes, and the food is still hot."

"I'm not hungry, dear. Let me change my dress, then I'll do the dishes. You go do your homework."

Pam hesitated. "Well—all right. I have lots to do."

"Lots? That doesn't sound like my intelligent Pam. Can't you keep up with the country children?" Paul's lightness masked only thinly a malicious pleasure.

Pam said quietly, "I've done mine. I'm doing some for other kids now. Writing themes for them."

Paul said sharply, "That doesn't sound honest."

"I have to," Pam told him, in the same quiet tone. "In the gang, you have to help each other."

"Well—" Paul said uncertainly.

Pam went upstairs.

Susan, in her weariness, forgot to be clever and bide her time. "Now you have some idea of what goes on in New Harmony. Children are taught to cheat for each other."

"Oh, don't start exaggerating, just because Pam is writing a few exercises for someone. I hope she does not get caught at it, though. It would look bad."

"Is that your standard? Do anything dishonest—it's all right, so long as you don't get caught!"

"Of course that is not my standard! What's wrong with you?"

"One of the reasons I went into Franklin today was to see if you were working overtime—or having an affair with Olivia Belgrove. I sat in the park opposite her home most of the afternoon. That was quite a farewell scene, with Olivia in her black negligee!"

"*What!*"

Paul's face went bright red. He stared at her with eyes wide and dark.

Susan leaned forward against the back of a chair. She was so tired. Every nerve and muscle in her body cried out for rest.

"And please don't tell me you were discussing business with her. I'm not a child. I've been aware that you've been seeing her steadily since last spring."

"Now, Susan, you mustn't jump to—Oh, what's the use?" He turned away.

"She's the reason you moved us out here to this desolate place, so you could be free to carry on your affair. Are you planning to leave us here and marry her? Because I don't intend to stay here. I won't stand for—"

"No!" He whirled. "I never meant that! I never meant to leave you and the children! Believe me, it was not that."

"What then? Surely you don't deny the affair. It's obvious enough."

"I know. I know. I meant to stop long ago. I never meant to let it go on this long. It's just that she—she keeps calling me. I never knew anyone like her. She's so beautiful, and wealthy. She has had everything. She is at the top of society. Yet she keeps wanting me! I can't understand it."

Susan stared at her husband. She had never heard before such an admission of weakness from him.

"She's exciting, and different. When she first asked me to come out to the house, I could not believe my luck. She was—I never felt like that before. Believe me, Susan, I never meant to let it go on."

"She persuaded you to buy the house here."

"It was a bargain! I got it for half the price."

"And forced us to move here, to this desolate, Godforsaken mudhole—"

"Now, look, Susan, I admit I'm having a fling with a woman. But that doesn't alter the fact that this house is a bargain, and that move was a smart one. Living in the country is good for the children."

"The hell it is," said Susan.

Paul flung down her jacket. It landed on a dining room chair. "You're upset about Olivia. I never meant to leave you and marry her, believe me! But it's mainly your fault it's gone on so long."

"My fault!" Oh, surely, he couldn't blame her for this! She could barely speak—she was so angry.

"I meant to break it off long ago. But you've slept alone practically the whole time since we moved. Damn, I'm human! You can't blame me for giving another woman what you refused!"

"Really, Paul, this is too much! You're not going to make me shoulder the blame for your affair!"

"It's true. I would have stopped long ago. But you wouldn't let me touch you, you wouldn't come to bed with me. And every time I came home, all you did was argue and make a fuss about this house, this neighborhood. You can't blame me for trying to find a woman who was more—more womanly."

The front door banged. Harvey came in. "Hi, Mom! You're late."

"Where have you been?" she asked sharply.

"Out with the gang—the fellows, I mean."

"What were you doing?"

He shrugged uneasily, not meeting her eyes. "Aw, just messing around."

"Have you had supper?"

"Naw."

"Neither have I. I'll fix you something." Susan went out to the kitchen, not bothering to change her good suit skirt, and fixed sandwiches and milk for Harvey. She was so furious at Paul that she did not want to speak to him again. The gall of him, to blame her for his affair!

She did the dishes, then went to bed early, ignoring Paul. She was so tired, it was hard to get to sleep. Then she overslept Sunday morning.

It was raining hard when she wakened. The sky was completely overcast with dirty grey clouds, and the rain poured down in a dreary monotony. She watched the rain dripping down the windows, the trees swaying in the downpour.

When she finally got up, she found the children reading quietly in the front room. Paul had overslept also, and was not up yet. He did not get up till noon.

She was coldly polite to Paul at dinner. The children could sense the tension in the air, and were uneasy.

After dinner, Paul followed Susan out to the kitchen. The children were in the front room. He closed the kitchen door.

"You've got to listen to me, Susan. It isn't fair to accuse me of all sorts of things when I'm not guilty."

"You are guilty. You are having an affair with Olivia Belgrove."

"It's over! That's what you wouldn't let me tell you. That's why I came home last night instead of staying all weekend. I told her it was over. I'm not going back."

"So that makes you not guilty?" she demanded angrily.

He came up close behind her and put his big hands on her waist. She hated for him to touch her at that moment. It was hard to keep up her anger when his touch turned her to liquid fire inside.

"Listen, darling, you are the one I love. I don't love her! I would never leave you. I love you too much. It was just a fling, as I said. If you had slept with me this summer—"

She jerked herself away. "There you go, blaming me again! When are you going to start accepting the blame for your mistakes?"

"My mistakes! You're as much to blame as I am! You've changed, Susan. You're not the sweet girl I married."

"It's about time I learned to be tough. People who are gentle and weak just get trampled on," she told him bitterly.

"When have I ever trampled on you?" He was hard to resist when he used that sweet, winning tone. "I've always tried to protect you, as much as I could. You don't know how harsh the world can be."

"I'm learning—here in New Harmony! Where my son has to learn to fight, my daughter has to learn to cheat—"

He flung out of the kitchen and slammed the door behind him. They quarreled again later in the afternoon. Paul seemed to realize at last that Susan was not the meek person she had been once, and that she was not going to be pacified easily. They quarreled about Olivia, about the move to New Harmony, about the unwholesome influences on Pam and Harvey.

The only subject Susan did not bring up was that of her prospective job. She railed at herself as a coward, but she could not bring herself to speak the words.

The children went to bed early that night, as though glad to easape the tensions of the household for a while. Paul seized on the opportunity to try to win her over.

"Look Susan," he said in his most charming way. "We don't get anywhere by quarreling. Just try me out. I've promised to give up Olivia. See if I don't! You won't have to worry any more, I swear it."

"And what about leaving New Harmony, going back to Franklin?" she demanded.

His face hardened. "So you're going to use the affair to club me into moving back to Franklin! Well, that won't work. This place is best for the children, and we are going to stay here. The country is best for them, Susan. When I was a boy, it made a world of difference to me, leaving that ugly city house and moving out to the farm. I was a changed person.

"But that was different—"

"No, it is not. I grew up in the country, Susan, and even though I am foreign born, I can go anywhere, have dinner with the best people. People respect me, Susan! How could that be if the country is so bad for people?"

"Oh, Paul," she said helplessly. She had never realized this weakness of his so keenly, the longing to be accepted in society. He was still the shy immigrant, taking an awed delight in being welcomed wherever he went. In a flash of insight she understood his affair with Olivia. He would not have been attracted into an affair with a secretary, or a middle-class girl. No. He had had the affair with Olivia Belgrove to prove to himself—and the world— that he was capable of keeping a wealthy and aristocratic woman as his mistress.

He pulled her over to the couch and drew her down on his knees before she realized what he was doing. But I mustn't, she thought desperately.

"Darling," he whispered. "I love only you. I'll prove it—I'll show you—"

He kissed her mouth, pulled her closer in his arms and tilted back her head. He kissed her chin, her throat, burying his face against her. He used his strength to subdue her feeble struggles.

"No, Paul, I don't want—"

"It's been so long," he said passionately. "You haven't let me touch you for so long."

His hands were weakening her, his big, clever hands pressing her hips, her waist. He opened her dress and put his mouth against the silk of her slip, over her breasts. She stiffened, then as he went on kissing her, she sighed and went limp. His touch was so familiar, yet so strange. It was so long since he had kissed her.

She went with him to his bedroom. His hands were quick and eager and skillful in undressing her. She remembered he had done this often in the early years of their marriage. More recently, he had taken her too much for granted.

When she lay naked on the bed, he undressed himself, and lay down beside her.

"The light," she murmured, as he turned her toward him.

He laughed, deep in his throat. "No. I want to see you."

His hands moved over her, awakening familiar memories without erasing the new. If he took her swiftly, and left her, she vowed she would go right back to her room.

But he had learned some lessons this summer. He was teasing and sure of himself in arousing her. He moved with accustomed precision that reminded her of their courtship, reducing her to helpless, rapt submission. He lingered long over her, his hands caressing her breasts, holding her waist and hips in sure confident caresses. In spite of her willful determination not to yield easily, she found herself stirred, moving helplessly under his directon, then suddenly violently convulsed, curling up on him, collapsed on him.

He held her tightly, whispering wild words to her. "You adorable—come to me—little cat—curl up here—let me love you—"

He turned her over on her back. He was still unsatisfied, still wanting to play, he smiled down at her in excitement.

And she felt a fresh emotion.

She was afraid of him, this big man who could control her mind, her emotions, her body. She shut her eyes tightly. She felt him come at her hotly, like a roused tiger, driving at her, driving into her emotions, into mutual memories, higher, deeper, painfully far. She cried out, tried to slide away from him. His hands grasped her waist, held her cruelly.

He was using her like a mistress, like Olivia, she thought as she fought him weakly. This was the way he had treated Olivia this summer, like a tiger stalking its prey, pouncing, tearing, ravishing.

He was too much for her, forcing her to yield to his strength, using her to please himself. But just when she would have screamed and torn herself from his cruelty, he bent and kissed her breasts, her waist, so sweetly that she caught her breath. Her heart yielded to him. She lay still and let him go on caressing her even after she lay exhaused

Then the change came in her. As her mental resistance melted, her body seemed to melt also, accept him, and their one-time closeness. She lay relaxed under him, the pain no longer painful, his needs fitted to hers now. As he stroked her slowly her emotions rose to match his and memory of their early love helped her to physical fulfillment.

She felt bathed in liquid fire, drowned in volcanic lava.

He slid off her, crouched above her, smiling down at her.

"You liked that, didn't you? I knew you would." His hand touched her waist, slid down to her hips. "There is a lot of passion there I had not found before. I knew I could find it."

He bent and kissed her body wildly. He was so aroused that he wanted her again soon. He did not seem like the husband she had known before, satisfied with a quick embrace, then rolling over to sleep. She scarcely knew what to think of him. She found herself thinking that if Olivia had taught him this, she should be grateful to her ...

He made love to her four times with scarcely a pause between embraces. He seemed surprised that she could meet his passion with an equal passion.

"We have not really known each other, Susan," he said, as he finally lay back to rest. "If you had been like this before—"

She stiffened. There he was, blaming her again.

He finally turned off the light, and came back to bed. She thought to go to sleep at once, but instead he was at her again, as though the darkness had renewed his sexual powers. He satisfied himself twice more, before he finally relaxed and lay back to go to sleep.

She could not sleep. She lay awake for a long time, listening to the steady drumming of the rain on the windows.

Finally she got up, gathered her clothes in her arms, and crept quietly back to bed in her own bedroom.

What was bothering her? She should feel tired and satisfied over this reconciliation with Paul. If he loved her like this, she ought to be able to persuade him before long to make the move back to Franklin.

Duane! That was what bothered her. She had taxed Paul with his infidelity. But she had been just as guilty with Duane. She had lain with the boy, enjoyed his embraces, yet had no intention at all of leaving Paul and marrying Duane. This too had been a fling for her, a boost for her ego.

She was angry at herself for her looseness. Why hadn't she had strength enough to resist having an affair with Duane? She was as bad as Paul. She had used Duane—she had enticed a young boy to her bed.

He had enjoyed it, yes. If she had suggested breaking it off in all earnestness, he had been equally sincere in wanting to continue the affair. He had loved their embraces. Yet they had been wrong.

She lay and tossed restlessly, wide awake for most of the night. Toward dawn she fell into a light sleep, from which she jerked awake at the sound of Pam's alarm clock.

It was Monday, another day, the beginning of another week. And her problems seemed more impossibly complex and insoluble than ever.

CHAPTER TWELVE

PAUL managed to find a moment alone with Susan before he left for the city. "Why did you leave my bed last night?" he asked curtly.

"I couldn't sleep," she replied, not meeting his gaze.

He shrugged, and said something about women being illogical.

Finally all three of them had left the house, and she was alone with her tormented thoughts. Was she to blame for Paul's affair, as he had said? How ridiculous! Before they had moved to New Harmony, they had slept in the same bed all their married years. It was only after the affair had begun, after Paul had forced the move from the city, that Susan had begun sleeping in another room.

No, there was something more deeply wrong than that between them. There was a lack of faith, of confidence, of loyalty.

Duane came over early, his boyish face eager. "What happened Saturday? Did you get the job?"

The job? It took a moment to remember. So much had happened since then.

"Oh. The job. Yes, Mr. Crandall offered me the job. He was very nice, very kind."

"Well, did you take it? You did, didn't you?" His kind face was puzzled.

"Not exactly. I told him I'd have to think it over. I'll have to tell—to ask—to tell Paul."

"Gosh, didn't you tell him this weekend, so you can start right in?"

"No, it isn't as simple as all that." She sighed heavily, and sat down at the kitchen table.

He watched her with interest and sympathy. "I wish I could help."

She shook her head. "It's too complex. Duane, I must tell you something." She nerved herself to say the cruel words. "Our affair has got to stop. It isn't right. We mustn't go to bed together any more."

His face immediately showed his hurt. "Why not? What happened?"

"Nothing has happened. Not yet. But it isn't right, and we must stop."

"I don't want to stop till we have to."

"We'll have to soon anyway."

"Let's wait then. Can't we go to your room now? And I want to hear all about the job too."

It was hard to refuse. She wanted very much to go to bed with him, to talk things over with him. But that was weakness, as weak as Paul's going to bed with Olivia.

"No, Duane. Not any more. And I've got work to do."

He stood up and came behind her chair. He put his hands on her shoulders, then slid them down to her breasts squeezing and caressing her. The touch turned her limp. She was becoming too accustomed to his love-making—he could arouse her too readily.

"Don't, Duane!" she said, more sharply than she had meant to. "Don't touch me!"

His hands dropped from her at once. He turned and went outside.

She sat at the table, her face in her hands. Now she had hurt him, this gentle, kind boy who had never hurt her, who never wanted to hurt anybody. It did no good to tell herself that he must be hurt sooner or later. She wanted to call him back.

But it was ended, this bittersweet romance with a boy so much younger than she, who had given her so much love and adoration.

Finally she got up and went over to the sink to do the dishes.

"Oh, Duane," she breathed. She saw him from the window. He was working in the backyard, raking the leaves, piling them into baskets. As she watched he picked up a heavy basketful and started back to the trash pile.

He was doing her work, even though she had turned him away. Even though she had rejected him, his devotion was unchanged. He was better to her than Paul was. He loved her with more single-mindedness, more adoration, more unselfishness than her own husband.

When he came back with the empty basket, she called to him. He came to the back door.

"Do you want something, Susan?"

"Yes. I've changed my mind. The hurt can come later."

"You mean—"

"I want you with me now," she said.

He was not slow in coming in. He held her and kissed her hard, wrapping his long arms around her. It was good to feel his lithe young body pressing against hers.

They went to her room.

He seemed to sense her weariness by lover's instinct, and was gentle with her, drawing her to him with tender hands.

He seemed to want to kiss and caress her, most of all. He stroked her body tenderly, touching the breasts, holding each in a big palm, smoothing the nipple with his thumb.

Even when he wanted her, before long, and made himself a part of her, he was slow and gentle. He drew the experience out, lying lazily with her, in a silence as deep as the quiet world that surrounded them. She caressed the blond head that lay on her breast, weaving her fingers into the short curls.

They were glad to be together, not moving, not speaking, only holding and caressing and feeling the nearness and warmth of each other.

Finally Duane raised up and drew himself away a little from her, looking at her with loving anxiety. She felt he wanted to ask what was wrong, but was too shy, too thoughtful to ask. She smiled at him to show she was not upset or angry, and with her hands on his waist she drew him back to her.

This time she wanted passion, and he gave it to her, in hard brutal caresses—deep delightful pleasures that thrust her out of her depression and made her forget everything but the joy of being in his embrace once more. With his newly-acquired skill, he built them both to ecstasy, until she had to respond fully to him, and cry out her pleasure.

He completed the embrace.

Then he drew off, and lay down beside her again, and pulled her over to lie in the bend of his thin body, his legs behind hers, his hips curved to hers, his heart beating steadily somewhere near her ears. She sighed with delight, and took his hand and cupped it around her breast.

She must have gone right off to sleep. She was only vaguely aware of his body next to hers, his hand holding her breast, the heartbeat that was so firm and reassuring. She awakened some time later to find him kissing her shoulders, her arms, her waist.

"Oh, I was asleep."

"Yes. It's nearly twelve. I decided to kiss you awake." His grin was boyish, but his caresses were now mature and daring. She lay still and let him venture where he pleased. She did not want to stop him.

When he left her that day, and went to work at the store, she watched him walk down the highway toward town. What a wonderfully sweet person he was! She did not want to hurt him at all. Yet he must, inevitably, be hurt. They could not go on forever like this.

That night, when Paul was ready to go to bed, he asked her to come with him.

Susan was taken off guard. She had not dreamed Paul would want her again so soon. They had not slept together all summer. Before that, he had been a supremely indifferent lover. Now, to want her two nights in a row was inconsiderate of him. She had not counted on it. And she was limp from the hours in bed with Duane.

"Oh, no!" she said without thinking. "I can't possibly—"

"Can't!" said Paul, outraged. "Are you such a frail woman you can't sleep with your husband more than once a year?"

"I'm still pretty tired from last night," she said with false meekness.

He stamped off to bed alone, and she let him go with a feeling of cold triumph. This was one time when he would not dominate her.

That night she slept well. When she wakened in the morning, it was with a new thought: she was changing. Meek, frightened, timid, dependent Susan was finding a will of her own.

For years she had depended on her mother. Then, as she began to work her way through college, she was just on the verge of becoming self-confident when Paul came along—strong, dominant, powerful. In her admiration and love, she had allowed herself to be ruled by him—sinking back into the submissive, obedient girl's role she had played before. It was so much easier to let other people make decisions, and so much easier not to fight for what one believed and wanted.

Duane was helping to free her, she thought, as she got up and dressed. In his admiration, his desire for her, he made her feel like a woman, not like a girl to be played with in a few idle moments.

Her hands paused. She stared unseeingly at her shoe. Yes, Paul had treated her like one of the children, a little more than Pam, a little less than Harvey. She was treated like a young girl, not smart enough to be trusted, not intelligent enough to be consulted, not mature enough to be considered as a half of a team. She was a child, to be amused, to be played with in one's spare time!

She tried to see Paul's side of it: all the women he had known had "left" him. His mother had died when he was a boy. His aunt, his new guardian, had been killed in an automobile accident. Perhaps he thought of women as fragile, temporary beings, not to be counted on.

Paul was a hard man, a clever, resourceful person. It was difficult to know him. She had a feeling that Paul did not really know himself. He was fighting blindly in the world, kicking out first before he could be kicked. He probably had no idea how he hurt Susan and the children by his indifferent manner, or his rough words.

Why couldn't he have turned out like Duane? Duane had been neglected, treated with callousness and indifference. She had learned that much about him and his relationship to his mother. But Duane had not reacted with hate, nor tried to fight the world. He sought love, and gave it eagerly.

Where would their relationship end? If she went back to Franklin, as she was determined to do, that would end the affair at once. Would Duane be cruelly hurt? She did not want that. She did not want to hurt him.

After Paul and the children had left for the day, Duane came over.

He said, "I'll help you with the housework today. I didn't give you much time to work yesterday."

"Let's not," she said recklessly. "We may not have much time. If I go back to Franklin—Well, I won't care if this house is clean or not! Let's go to bed."

He laughed, gleefully. "Okay! You don't have to talk me into it."

They went upstairs at once, and undressed. She thought, how familiar and easy it had become. Yet how desperate she felt when she thought each time might be the last. She did not want to leave him.

Some time later in the day, Duane said the same thing. "I keep thinking each time this might be the last. And I have the feeling that maybe if I ever marry, I might not be lucky enough to get a woman like you. She might not know—be as wise as you are. You don't really mind, do you? When I play at love? You like it, don't you?"

She had to confess she enjoyed it, thoroughly. She felt so uninhibited with him, so free from restraint or censure.

On Wednesday he came again, and again they went to bed together. Each had the feeling that it could not last, and they were greedy to drain the last sweet drops of emotion and excitement from their relationship. Duane outdid himself in inventing new embraces, caressing her in wildly imaginative fashions.

Duane said, "I wonder if other people ever have such fun."

"I doubt it," said Susan. "People are too inhibited. Or they're too busy making money. As if money was more fun than this."

"I wonder if I'd learn more about this at college," he asked another time.

Susan chuckled. "Ha! I can imagine a college course in this! It would be the most popular course ever taught!"

But always in their joy was a sense of frantic hurrying, of worry, of dread. This time might be the last. So hurry, snatch it, make it terribly sweet, drain every last drop of love.

There was no time for lingering, no time to pet and caress slowly and draw it out lazily. No time for that any more. Time was fleeting. Time was swift. And one could not cheat time. It caught up before one knew.

The delicious embraces would be over, the touching of hands, the lingering of mouths, the entwining of bodies, the final wild ecstacies. All, all would be over, and they would be apart.

And even the memory would fade, because memories do fade and change. From the moment he left, or she did, the memory would change until there was little truth left, and no clear remembrance of how it had been between them. All each would know was, "For a short time, I loved, and was loved."

CHAPTER THIRTEEN

PAUL had been curt and brusk since Monday night when Susan had refused to go to bed with him. On Thursday afternoon, he phoned to say briefly that he was staying in town that night to work.

"To work—or see Olivia?" Susan demanded agrily.

"Don't be a jealous fool."

"Look here, Paul, you said that was over!"

"I can't talk now," said Paul, his tone suddenly smooth and soft. Someone must have come into his office. "Goodbye, Susan."

He hung up before she could say another word. She smarted with anger when she realized he was probably headed for Olivia's house. She sat at the phone and fumed. Should she call him back and bawl him out?

Maybe he was going to work overtime. She would wait and see. Tonight she would call the office, then the apartment. If he was not at either place, she would call Olivia's house.

She was so angry at Paul, it was difficult to think of anything else. Pam brought her friend Carol Emmert home from school with her to see how the formal looked on Pam. Susan felt impatient with both girls. Coral had come with Pam after school on Monday to see the formal. She had come after school on Tuesday to decide on makeup. She had come after school on Wednesday to discuss whether blue was right for Pam after all.

Susan had visions of herself dashing into Franklin Saturday to exchange the formal for Pam's dance that night. The way the two girls worried over one dress and one dance, one might think it was the most important social event of the season.

She tried to curb her impatience. After all, to Pam it was the most important event of the year—her first dance with a date. She would think her whole future depended on her success at the dance. Susan vowed grimly that before a second dance could take place, Pam would be back at Franklin, out of this unwholesome atmosphere.

The girls came in from school. Harvey had walked along behind them all the way home, and seemed to feel he had had enough of their chatter. He dropped his books in the living room and went right out again, to "mess around with the gang."

That too would stop soon. Back in Franklin, Harvey would be with his old friends again, the ones interested in scientific experiments and ham radios and books.

Pam and Coral went off together. They were gone so long and were so quiet that Susan finally became concerned and went to Pam's room.

As soon as she came near the closed door, she smelled smoke—cigarette smoke. She tapped on the door.

"Come in!" said Pam.

Coral was sitting on the bed, smoking a cigarette. She did not bother to hide it or put it out. Pam was standing before the mirror, soberly staring at herself.

The girl looked all of sixteen. The vivid blue formal set off her dark hair and blue eyes, and the high heels made her seem taller. She wore makeup too old for her, but it showed how she would look in a few years—lovely, fresh, beautiful, poised. She wore the iridescent beads, and carried the blue velvet bag.

"Oh, Pam, you look lovely!" Susan exclaimed impulsively.

"Do you think so, Mummy? Coral says she's not sure this blue is right for me."

"She's young yet," drawled Coral. "The pastel blue would probably be better."

Susan was surprised, until she saw the flicker of Coral's eyes, her glance at Pam. Coral was jealous. She had had no idea her protegée would look so beautiful.

"Maybe you're right," said Susan placatingly; anything to get this first dance over with! "She looks quite pretty, though. I think it might be all right. Or do you think I ought to exchange it?"

"Maybe you ought to. Maybe get something green," said Coral, puffing violently on her cigarette.

Green was Pam's worst color. Suan wanted to laugh. But she must be tactful and cautious until Pam was well away from the jealous girl.

"Well, it'll be hard to get into Franklin again," said Susan, pretending to think hard. "Perhaps this dress will do for the first dance, then next time—"

Coral finally departed, and Pam burst into tears.

"Oh, Mummy, she didn't like the dress!"

Susan patted her shoulder. A few months ago she would have let Pam sob on, and comforted her ineffectually. Now she felt years older and more worldly-wise. It was better to give Pam the truth and help her face reality.

"No, she didn't like it. It was too beautiful. It makes you look so much lovelier than she could ever be. She's jealous."

Pam's tears stopped. "Jealous!" she gasped.

"Exactly. She never realized you could outshine her so easily. But be careful, Pam! She's a tough girl, and she can hurt you if she gets angry with you. Don't let any of her boy friends be attracted to you if you can help it."

"Oh, Mummy!"

Susan had never spoken to Pam like this before. No wonder the girl was bewildered.

"We're going to leave New Harmony soon, Pam," Susan went on. "So if you and Harvey can stick it out for a couple more weeks, then I'll have you back in Franklin where you'll be safe."

Pam was staring at her in wild hope. "Oh, Mummy, are we going to move back? Did Daddy say so?"

"Not yet, but he will!" said Susan grimly, recalling Paul's behavior today.

Pam looked down at her dress. "Oh," she said, her voice becoming cool, doubtful. "Well, we'll see what happens. Do—do you think I ought to get another dress, one that Coral won't be jealous about?"

"No. That one looks lovely. Just don't take any boy friends away from her. Is she especially fond of anyone?"

"Fred Goss. But he won't look at me. He's sixteen."

"Just be careful," said the new, harder Susan. Paul would not be home. Harvey would not be back till dark.

She sat down with her daughter and proceeded to tell her some facts of life that she needed for survival in New Harmony. Susan was not sure herself where she had learned this wisdom, but she was only sorry she had not helped Pam more when they first came.

"Be sure to stay with your date," she concluded. "Merv is a nice boy and he won't try to make trouble. Don't let anyone try to take you out after the dance. Just say you appreciate their kindness, but you're very tired and are going home."

"But Coral might not like it!"

"Be careful of what Coral likes. It's just about certain to be the wrong thing. She hasn't started you smoking, has she?"

"Not yet," said Pam. "She says I should start soon, or the boys will think I'm queer."

"Put it off. Keep putting it off. We'll be out of this place before long."

"Daddy doesn't think so," said Pam simply. "And he's the one who decides, isn't he?"

"I'm going to change his mind," said Susan, "if it's the last thing I do."

Pam was not reassured. She looked ready to burst into tears again. "Oh, Mummy, please don't fight with him! It's so terrible. I can get along here. Don't worry. I'll get along all right. Just don't fight with him."

Susan said, "I don't like fighting. I've always tried to avoid a fight. But once in a great while, if you don't fight, you lose everything you believe in. You have to fight—and win. This time, I'm fighting."

"Oh, Mummy!" Pam started to cry. "I don't want you to fight. I don't want you to."

"Don't worry about that," said Susan. "You just concentrate on living through these next couple of weeks. Then I'll have you out of here."

She left Pam to change back to her simpler clothes, and went to start supper. She felt heady with her own advice. Fight! She'd have to fight, and win, and get the children back to Franklin.

All through supper, while Pam sat subdued and frightened, and Harvey seemed strangely quiet, Susan planned what she would say to Paul. For once in her life she felt angry, ready for a good rousing fight. And she certainly had an issue to fight over.

She waited till the children had gone to their rooms to do their homework. Their homework, she thought, in hard disgust. Pam was composing themes for stupid friends of Coral. Harvey was copying out arithmetic problems and answers for "friends" of his.

First she phoned Paul's office. As she had expected, there was no answer. Then she had the operator call the apartment where he stayed overnight—or said he did. No answer there, though the phone rang and rang.

She gave the operator Olivia's number. "If they say he isn't there, tell them it's an emergency call. I must reach him."

"Yes, ma'am."

The operator dialed. Someone answered, probably a maid. "The Belgrove residence."

"Mr. Paul Wladek, please. Long distance calling," said the operator.

The girl hesitated. "Oh—there's no one here by that name, I don't believe, operator."

"It's an emergency," said the operator. "I've been trying to reach this party. Do you know where he can be located?"

"Excuse me, operator. Just a minute."

There was a long wait, then Paul came to the phone.

"Hello?"

"Mr. Paul Wladek?" asked the operator.

"Yes. Yes. What's wrong?"

"Go ahead, please," said the operator.

"Hello, Paul," said Susan.

"Susan? What's wrong? What's the emergency?"

She heard the click as the operator closed her key.

"I thought I'd find you at Belgrove's!" she said angrily. "You said it was all over, and there you are again!"

"Wait, Susan! What's the emergency? Is Pam—"

"Pam's crying, but you wouldn't care about that. The children are in their rooms, doing homework for other children. Cheating! But you wouldn't care about that. That's part of the healthy wholesome country atmosphere!"

"Susan, will you get to the point! What's wrong!"

"You're wrong!" she screamed. "You're a liar and a cheat! That's why you want your children to be liars and cheats! You're an adulterous, conniving, scheming, lying bastard!"

"Is there any emergency?" Paul's voice had turned very cold and hard.

"Yes! An extreme emergency! We want to move out of this horrible place as soon as possible. If you don't—"

Click. He had hung up. Susan started to cry, with rage and frustration. The operator came back on the line.

"Is the call completed, ma'am?"

"Yes," sobbed Susan. "It's finished." She hung up.

She had all the proof she needed. If Paul did not move them back to Franklin, she was through with him. She would take the job, and move herself and the children back to Franklin, in spite of Paul.

She was through believing him, or respecting his judgment. And she would not allow the children to be corrupted in New Harmony, just to leave Paul to carry on his affair in peace.

CHAPTER FOURTEEN

SUSAN shook with rage all evening as she recalled the phone conversation. There was something about blowing up at Paul, releasing her pent-up rage, that served to increase her anger instead of diminishing it.

On Friday, she and Duane went to bed again, as usual, but she did not find her usual pleasure in their intense love-making. She was so busy rehearsing in her mind what terrible things she would say to her husband, what threats she would make, what promises to leave him if he did not move them back to Franklin, that she could not concentrate on Duane and his caresses.

He felt it, she knew, though he said nothing. He soon gave up trying to arouse her, and lay quietly holding her in his arms. She could almost forget he was there, except for the slight pressure of his hands as he moved them slowly over her breasts, her waist and hips. He seemed to be soothing her, rather than caressing her, and she felt comforted by his silent sympathy.

By noon, she felt calmed and more ready to forget Paul for a while. She turned to Duane and put her arms around his body.

"I'm sorry—wasting all that time," she said.

"When I'm with you, it isn't wasting time. All the other time is wasted."

When he left that day, he kissed her very sweetly. She touched his curly head with tender fingers, and tried to smile.

"I'm sorry," she murmured.

"Sorry? No need to be sorry. You're a wonderful woman."

"I didn't feel much—I couldn't—"

"I know. But you let me stay. It's good for me, if I can just see and touch you."

She smiled at him. "No more till Monday," she said regretfully.

"May I come then?"

"Yes. We'll have fun," she promised. "Lots of fun."

"And I'll learn more—"

"As much as you want—"

He kissed her, slowly. "I hate to leave you. You feel so good. You smell so good."

"You'll be late for work."

He had to pull himself away from her. He hated to leave, that was obvious.

She found after he left that she missed him. It had taken a while, but he had finally succeeded in helping her forget Paul and her quarrel with him. Now that Duane had gone, her thoughts crowded back.

This time her anger was cold.

Paul came home about five-thirty. He must have left work early, she thought. There was a white line of fury around his mouth. His voice was curt and he spoke little. He waited till supper was over.

Then he told the children, "Go to your rooms. Your mother and I have something to discuss."

Pam gave him a single terrified glance, and fled like a timid animal. Harvey trudged after her, taking things more stoically, as was his custom.

Susan had meant to start the argument and keep it on the lines she wanted, but Paul beat her to the punch.

"How vile can you be?" he demanded. "Calling me long distance, saying it was an emergency! Just to say you wanted to move back to Franklin. Were you drunk last night?"

"Not drunk. Furiously angry," said Susan coldly. "You had told me your affair with that dyed divorcée was over. I proved it was not, and I proved you're a liar."

He flushed, and counterattacked in another direction. "You have only yourself to blame. You wouldn't even sleep with me through one night! You refused me the next night."

"Coward!" she replied. "You're blaming me again for your filthy affair. I refuse to shoulder the blame any more."

"You are the one who is to blame for the affair—" he began.

She cut him short. "No, I'm not. You can twist your words around all you want. But I know the truth and I won't be intimidated any longer."

"The truth! You don't know what—"

"The truth is you moved us out here to clear the way for your affair. You refuse to move us back because you won't give up that woman. She caters to your ego. She makes you feel like a wealthy rotten bum, just as she is a wealthy rotten bitch."

"You shut your mouth about her! She is—"

Susan found strength she had never known she possessed. "I know what she is. Her history is common gossip. She had blue blood, yes, but no money. So she married a rich old man. When he refused to die soon enough for her, she divorced him for a big hunk of his money. Then she married her gigolo lover, only to find he was as unfaithful to her as she had been to her husband. So she wanted a divorce. But she didn't plan to pay him as she had been paid. Oh, no. She set up her innocent cousin, made it look like adultery, and dragged the poor girl through the divorce courts with her. Some sweet bitch, she is!"

"You're twisting the facts! Olivia is not like that!"

"She is. And I'm not going to sacrifice the futures of my children to satisfy her erotic instincts! This place is a rotten pesthole. If you ever stayed around here with your eyes open, you'd see it clearly, and not keep on claiming it's a sweet, fresh country place!"

"You've never liked the country—"

"I like the country, when it's really clean, and fresh, and unspoiled." Susan was surprised at herself, how calmly she could out-talk him, how quickly she could answer. "But this isn't. The gangs are not the black-jacketed juvenile delinquents of the city, that's true. They're amateurs. They're spoiled kids looking for thrills, neglected by society, ignored by the police, trying to be adults too fast. But they're dangerous all the same. And Pam and Harvey are not going to be forced to become like them!"

"You're wrong about this. And they are going to stay. This house was a bargain, and we're not going to move out because of your whims."

She played her ace. "We are—the children and I. We're going back to Franklin. You can stay here and keep house and smell the open sewers, and walk in the mud of the unfinished housing projects, and enjoy the company of the tough gangs that breed here. But I'm taking the children back home, back to Franklin."

"And just what do you think you'll live on? If you think you'll get one cent from me—"

"I'll have a job. I can support us."

"On the pay of a clerk-typist?" he demanded.

She stiffened proudly. "I would if I had to. But it so happens I've been offered a job as an assistant editor on a magazine, *Field and City Street.*"

"They must be crazy! You're no editor."

"I'm a photographer. They liked my photos, and said they'd teach me the rest."

"Your photos! Your little amateur efforts! You can't get away with that."

"I'm not trying to get away with anything. You never thought much of my pictures, but Mr. Crandall and the others liked them. They liked them a lot."

Paul stared at her incredulously. "An editor. By God, what next?"

She seized the opportunity to press her point. "So I can support the children, quite nicely. We'll move soon, back to an apartment. You can come with us or not as you choose."

"You mean divorce?" he demanded.

"Yes. I want a divorce," said Susan recklessly.

"Well, go ahead and get it! I'm not stopping you. But I'll tell you one thing. You'll never get the children. I'll fight that in court!"

"How can you? They're mine. And your affair is quite obvious."

"Maybe so, but it'll be impossible to prove anything in court. And you never were very smart, Susan. Don't you think I can beat you quite easily in court?"

She stared at him wildly, at his cold triumphant smile. "You can't—You can't take the children—" She had never dreamed he would do that.

"Oh, yes, I will! You try to get a divorce and I'll go to court if I have to—to take the kids away from you!"

"Mummy! Daddy! Don't fight! Don't fight!" Pam tumbled into the room, followed by Harvey. She flung herself into Susan's arms, sobbing wildly.

"Pam! Go back to your room!" Paul thundered.

"No, no! Don't be mad! We'll stay here! We will. But don't get a divorce!" Pam sobbed. Susan held her closely, fighting her own impulse to break down too. She could not bear to give up the children. Paul did not really want custody of them, but to punish her for leaving him he would take the children away.

The children cried all evening, Harvey in his room, Pam following Susan around. It hurt her to hear them. She had wanted to settle everything quietly, so they would not be hurt.

Now it seemed they would all be hurt, unless she could think of something. But her ace had been played and she had lost.

CHAPTER FIFTEEN

AFTER a long night's sleep, Susan felt more calm, and more unsure of herself. Now that her furious anger no longer buoyed her up, she was more concerned about what Paul would do. Would he really carry out his threat to take away the children, if she went through with a divorce?

He could be an implacable enemy. No one could ever convince him he was wrong. He thought it weakness to be generous over a matter of principle. He would take the children away if he could, even though he did not want the personal care of them. He would hire someone to look after them, rather than let her have them.

It was not worth it to her. Not her freedom, escape from this place, at the expense of losing the children.

And crazily enough, she still did not want to give up Paul, either. She did not really want a divorce. She could not imagine herself divorced from him, the marriage ties broken.

She wanted their anger and their differences to end, she wanted them to live together—in Franklin!—peaceably again. The children had always loved and respected Paul. They looked up to him. Their mother was weak and gentle and lovable. But Paul had to remain their strong protection against the world.

It was because this protection had failed them, these past few months, that they felt so driven and desperate. She must try to heal the wound of separation. Once Paul was over his infatuation with Olivia, and the blind spot about New Harmony, all could be mended again. If only it were not too late!

She felt a vague worry, a fear that she was afraid to put in words, about staying here much longer. Pam was trembling on the brink of danger. She was blindly following Coral's lead—and Coral was jealous of her. What couldn't Coral do to her, if she pleased?

Susan lay in bed, that early Saturday morning, worrying futilely about Pam and her dance. Paul tapped lightly at the door, and came in. He was still in pajamas.

He closed the door behind him and came over to sit down on the edge of the bed.

"Hello," he said.

"Hello," she said in relief.

He touched her cheek with a gentle hand. "I don't like to fight with you, Susan."

"I don't either."

"I should not have gone back to Olivia. But you made me angry—Oh, all right! I won't blame you," he added hastily. "But I was finished with it. I had not planned to go back."

"And now—?"

He bent over and kissed her mouth. "You are still the only woman I love," he whispered.

She could not help it—she loved his touch. He was the man she had loved for years. She put her arms around him and drew him down to her. "Oh, Paul, oh, Paul, I love you so."

"Let's not fight any more. You don't really want a divorce, do you?"

"No! I hate the idea."

"I don't want it either." He kissed her again, then drew back the blankets to get into bed with her. She turned to him with relief. This was the quiet, strong, yet gentle man she loved, the one she could lean on, depend on through all troubles.

He kissed and caressed her for a long time, before slipping the nightgown up from her hips and leaning over her. His familiar strength guided her, his dark face lay against her breast, and after their stormy passion was fulfilled, she was at peace with him.

Even so, she could not talk to him about moving back to Franklin. She knew the peace was fragile. She was at the end of her resources. She did not know how to accomplish the move now.

Merv's mother, Mrs. Weston, had called to suggest that Paul and Susan and Harvey come over to her place while the children were at the dance. She had invited several other couples. It would be nice to get acquainted, she had said.

Susan suggested it to Paul before they got up that morning. "It might be nice," she said. "Merv's taking Pam to the dance, you know."

"Oh, yes. Well, why don't we?" he said agreeably. "We might as well get to know our neighbors a whole lot better."

"We could stay till about ten. I told Pam I wanted her to come home by ten if possible."

"From her first date?"

"She's only twelve years old."

"Well, don't spoil her fun."

Paul was in a good mood that day. He teased Pam about her date till she was red with embarrassment. But she was evidently pleased and relieved to have the quarreling over. Paul played ball with Harvey, then the two of them worked on the leaves.

He came in, puffing, about the middle of the afternoon. "Susan, that is a big yard. I don't know how you've managed to keep it so nice."

"Duane has looked after it most of the time, until recently," she said mildly. "He's been too busy this past week to do anything with it."

She still felt enough of her cold anger with Paul to be wickedly pleased at how busy Duane had been. Yes, she and Duane had managed to keep busy that week!

"Well, you must not depend on him anyway. I ought to pay him for the work he has done."

"Oh, I wouldn't offer. He was being neighborly," she said hastily. "I think he might resent your trying to pay him."

There was a pause.

"Just as you say," Paul finally agreed.

Pam was happy and thrilled by the time she was dressed for the party. Paul stared at her and whistled as she came down the steps.

"Wonderful, Pam! You look very pretty!"

She blushed again. Merv gave her a corsage of roses, which delighted her. Merv was a sober-faced, shy boy with spectacles and a nervous tic. But at least he was not one of the tougher gang members, thought Susan.

She watched them go with renewed apprehension. Merv's father was driving them and would pick them up again. But still—

"Are you ready, Susan?" Paul demanded impatiently.

"Oh—yes, I'm ready." She was wearing a blue lace dress that matched the blue of her eyes. It was cut in a V both front and back, but it did not seem too dressy. Mrs. Weston had said the evening would not be formal.

Harvey looked nice in a new brown suit. Paul looked stunning and distinguished, as usual, she thought with a rush of pride. He did look wonderful, with his dark hair edged with grey at the temples, his keen dark eyes, his dark face and sensitive hands.

It was dark by the time they reached the Westons'. The house was brightly lighted. Mrs. Weston met them at the door, and Susan gave her her coat.

"Oh, you dressed up," cried Mrs. Weston, obviously dismayed.

"This?" murmured Susan, puzzled. Then she saw that her hostess was wearing a gaudy cotton dress in a mock-peasant style, and the other women there were in similar simple, informal dresses, of gay cotton or jersey.

Susan felt awkward and out of place the rest of the evening. The hostess kept them determinedly busy with games that Susan felt she had outgrown at fourteen. There were several children who seemed to be constrained and stiff. The women ended up in one corner of the living room, discussing children, the men in another corner discussing business and sports. And the children roamed restlessly around, trying—as the hostess admonished them—to "have fun."

Paul signalled Susan about ten o'clock. Susan managed to break away gracefully. Harvey was equally eager to leave. As soon as they got into the car, Paul said, "Tcha! So that is the high life in New Harmony. Susan, remind me to take you to the next concert in Franklin."

"Thank you. I'll go," she said promptly.

"What did you think of the party, Harvey?" asked Paul jovially. "Did you have fun?" His tone mocked Mrs. Weston.

"It was all right," Harvey said. He went up to his room as soon as he got home.

Susan waited in the front room. "Pam will be home soon. I'll just wait till she comes."

"Oh, come to bed," Paul urged. "She'll come back all right. If Merv is as dull as his father, she will be home early."

"I want to hear about the dance," Susan said obstinately.

He sighed. "All right, then. I'll make myself a drink. I want to wash out the taste of those concoctions. What were they?"

"I think I tasted gin," she said vaguely, peering out the window. Was that car stopping? No, it only slowed, then speeded up again.

"Your taste is more delicate than mine. Do you want a strong one?"

"Not as strong as yours."

He went out to the kitchen and came back in a few minutes with their drinks. She sipped hers, still peering out.

"Oh, come and sit down, Susan. You make me nervous. She won't come any sooner for all your watching."

She sighed, and went over to sit beside him on the couch. What could happen to Pam? She was with a nice, mild boy. Merv's father was going to pick them up. Nothing could happen …

Ten-thirty came and went. Paul made himself another drink. When it was finished, he wanted to go to bed.

"No, you go ahead. I can't sleep till she comes in."

"In the name of heaven, is this going to go on for years until Pam is married? Think of the sleep I will lose. Me, the stern father, waiting up night after night. Why, we'll frighten off all the boys for miles around. She will never get married."

She had to laugh at his description, but her worry was growing. Now it was eleven o'clock. The dance was to be over at ten.

Where was Pam?

"Want another drink?" asked Paul.

"No. No more."

"I don't, either," he said. "I've got other things in mind. Come on over here."

To placate him, she sat on his lap. It did feel good to rest against him, to feel his hard, eager kisses on her mouth, her throat. But he was soon anxious for more than kisses.

"Come on, darling, let's go to bed."

"It's after eleven-thirty. Oh, Paul, something's dreadfully wrong! I don't know why—I can feel it in my bones."

"What can go wrong? Maybe she stopped off at the Westons'. The party was still going on."

"Maybe."

He stroked his hand over her thigh, coaxingly. "You looked so pretty tonight. The prettiest girl there."

"All dressed up," she added wryly.

"You made the rest look like peasants." He sounded proud of her. He did not seem to realize that making other woman look like peasants was not the best way in the world to become popular in a community like New Harmony.

He laid her across his thighs and held her strongly as he bent over and kissed her. He nuzzled his head between her breasts, pushing back the lace.

They both heard the car stop outside.

"Good. Now we can go to bed," said Paul. "I was going to take you right there on the couch in another minute."

Heels clicked on the sidewalk. Susan got up, straightened her dress and her hair, went to the door. She wondered if Merv would come in, too. She was relieved to hear the car pull away. It ground hard, then raced down the highway. Funny—she had not thought Merv's father was a hot-rodder. He did not look the type.

She opened the door.

Pam came in, alone.

"Hello, Mummy."

"Pam, dear—did you have a good time?" Her sharp eyes saw that the dress was badly mussed around the young shoulders. The jacket was crumpled, and so was the full skirt. Pam's lipstick was smeared. When she came over to the light, her eyes seemed frightened and startled.

"Fine," said Pam. "I had a fine time."

"Sit down and tell us all about it," said Paul, more interested now. "My, you certainly look grownup."

Pam perched on the edge of a straight chair, crumpling her velvet bag between nervous fingers. "I danced a lot. Lots of boys asked me."

"Fine!" said Paul. "Is Merv a good dancer?"

"Not very good. But I didn't get to dance very much with him." Her eyes flickered away from theirs. She stared down at her handbag.

"Did Coral have a good time?" asked Susan.

"I—I guess so. The eighth-graders were in another room, you know."

"Who did you dance with?"

"Oh, lots of boys. You don't know their names!"

"Fred Goss?" asked Susan gently.

Pam's honest tongue had not learned to lie yet. "Yes. Yes, he danced with me."

"Quite a lot?"

"Yes."

"Who's Fred Goss?" asked Paul.

"An older boy," said Susan shortly. "He's sixteen, and runs one of the gangs."

"Sixteen! Well, he must have thought you were older than twelve."

"He knows how old I am," said Pam.

"Who brought you home?" asked Susan. If Pam had attracted Fred Goss away from Coral …

"Fred Goss. Merv was supposed to, but Fred said he would, and I was afraid he'd hurt Merv, so I said I'd go. Merve didn't like it, but—" she shrugged.

"You're a fast worker! Boys fighting over you already," said Paul heartily. "Well, let's go to bed."

Pam got up at once. "Yes. I'm awfully tired," she said. "Good night, Mummy. Good night, Daddy." She escaped down the hall. Susan heard her door bang shut.

Susan's heart was heavy. She pieced together the threads of the story: Pam had danced often with Fred, who was Coral's steady. Coral was in another room. Therefore, Pam had taken Fred away from Coral—and Coral would be madly jealous.

The dance had been over at ten. Fred had taken Pam home— from ten to almost twelve. They must have gone somewhere and parked. Pam, parked in a car with a sixteen-year-old boy! No wonder her dress was mussed, her lipstick smeared, her eyes frightened.

"Come on, Susan. Or are you putting me off again?" Paul had turned off the lights and locked the doors.

"No. I'm ready." She went with him.

But long after Paul was asleep, his arms lax around her, Susan was still awake and terrified. Her Pam, her child, had attracted this tough young man, a ruthless and spoiled young man.

How could Pam cope with a boy like that? She was completely inexperienced and trusting. She would be an easy prey for someone unprincipled, like Fred Goss.

And Coral— The very thing Susan had feared had happened. Coral's boy had deserted her for Pam. Her jealous fury must have been aroused. What kind of revenge would she take on Pam?

CHAPTER SIXTEEN

PAM seemed to have decided to say little more about the dance. Susan's anxious questions brought only monosyllabic answers. "Yes, the dance was fine." "Yes, I had a nice time." "Yes, Merv had a nice time."

On Monday she went back to school as usual. But she and Harvey walked slowly, with dragging steps. They were obviously reluctant to go.

Duane came over soon after they left. "Did you hear those guys last night?" he asked at once.

"Yes. Several boys wandering around the yard. I told Paul, but he didn't seem to think it was important."

"Hum." Duane frowned. "Wonder why they're hanging around. We'll see."

Susan heard the boys again that night. They were bolder, calling up at the windows. "Pam. Hey, Pam! Where are you, pretty Pam?" Then they laughed. Their voices were high and shrill, falsely sweet.

Susan spoke to Paul, but again he brushed it off impatiently. "It's just their way of teasing Pam, showing their interest in her. Boys are like that. If I tried to drive them away, they would just become angry."

The boys were there again each night for the next several nights, calling to Pam, and also to Harvey, seeming not to want answers. They were bolder in their remarks. Susan did not like it at all.

Duane was very concerned. "They're working up to something. It's almost Hallowe'en. They play pretty rough around here on Hallowe'en."

"I don't care if they rip the yard and house to pieces! Just so they let Pam and Harvey alone!" Susan told him vehemently.

"I don't know. I wish I could find out what they're up to. But nobody will open up with me. They know I'm—interested in you."

"What about Coral Emmert? She hasn't come home with Pam all week."

"She's jealous. And it looks like Fred Goss did like Pam better than her. I think she's probably burning."

Susan sighed in frustration. She and Paul were sleeping together again. He was passionate, amorous, as he had not been in years. She had hoped that soon he would be willing to listen to her about moving back to Franklin. But she could not begin the subject without being cut off abruptly. Paul would not discuss the matter.

Meantime, the children were miserable and scared. Something was definitely brewing, but they would not talk to her about it.

She found comfort in Duane's arms. She lay with him every morning; their embraces were long and warm. In spite of her nights with Paul, she found she had energy and desire in plenty for Duane. She had given up trying to understand herself.

On Thursday morning, she was especially worried. The boys had been annoyingly persistent the night before, and Pam had finally broken down and wept. Even Paul had been concerned.

"You must not let them upset you," he had told Pam. "They're only teasing you. If they did not like you, they would not bother."

"They hate me!" Pam sobbed. "You don't know, Daddy. You don't know how they are."

"Of course I know. I was a boy myself. Why, I can remember—"

Pam wept, "You don't understand! You don't know! Oh, I wish I was dead!"

She fled to her room and locked herself in. Paul would not let Susan go to her.

"No, let her alone. She will feel better. And she has to learn to accept teasing."

"It isn't just teasing, Paul. You don't realize what kind of boys these are!"

He had not listened to her. Now she told Duane, "I'm sick with worry. We must leave here. Yet I can't convince Paul with words. He's so stubborn. Oh, what can I do? I'm really scared now."

Duane soothed her, but she knew he was deeply worried too. If Duane, knowing the kids, thought something bad would happen, it probably would. And how could she prevent it alone?

"Ready, darling?" Duane asked eagerly, after a time.

She pushed away troublesome thoughts, and smiled up at him. "Whenever you want."

She sighed with luxurious anticipation as he leaned over her, his left arm sliding under her neck. Her head fell back under his kisses; he buried his face in her throat. She could feel the rise of hot desire in herself, and the matching desire rising in him.

After he had adjusted himself over her, he drew back a little, raised up on his knees and looked down at her with a curious gaze, studying her naked body open for him. She was reminded of their first morning together, his curiosity, his joy, his enchantment with seeing as well as touching her.

She put her arms up behind her head, stretching out her body. He put his hands on her thighs, still staring at her with intent green eyes.

This time there was no need for music.

She smiled again, and moved to a more comfortable position, stretching slowly like a cat. She closed her eyes as he caressed her. He was so young yet, for all his masculinity. She hoped he would keep that youthful curiosity all his life. What pleasure he would give to a wife! She would be the luckiest girl in the world.

He had stopped kissing her. He leaned farther up over her, his face intent, scowling. He was no longer to be satisfied with kisses.

She stiffened for a moment, a sort of delicious terror in her. Sometimes this first part of the attack was terrifying. He might hurt her, rip her apart, destroy her.

Then she felt the dear familiarity of his hands on her, holding her steady, and the warmth of his thighs on hers. She relaxed and let him come up.

Something about the way he embraced her reminded her again vividly of their early days together. Was it because their parting must come soon?

After they were finished, and he lay beside her, she told him, "Duane, you ought to be thinking about your future."

"I like what's happening now better," he said, his hand cupping one full breast. She turned her head to watch his finger teasing the nipple.

"I know. But the future comes too fast. You ought to be ready. I want you to go to college, Duane."

"Can they teach me more about this?" he grinned.

She laughed. "No. But there's so much you should learn. And I want you to move away from here. Move to a city where there's a good college."

"I'd like to, sometime. Not now."

"You shouldn't wait. The longer you wait, the harder it'll be to go."

"Not now." He leaned over to kiss her breast. His lips caught the nipple and he bit it softly, then pulled on it strongly.

"But soon, Duane," she urged, catching his head in her hands and caressing his cheeks and his hair. "You will go soon."

"I won't leave you. As long as you're here, I'm going to stay."

"I want to leave soon. You know that."

"I'll wait."

She ran her fingers through the blonde curls. When she left, she would not see him any more. How incredible it seemed to her, lying naked under him, touching his head, his bare thin shoulders, that after a short time she would not be seeing him any more. Surely they could go on forever, caressing, embracing, desiring, fulfilling.

No. It would end. They would go their separate ways, each happier and sadder for the sweet experience. She clasped his body convulsively.

"Oh, I don't want to let you go!" she cried.

He raised his head, to look into her eyes. "I want to stay with you."

"It isn't possible."

"I know." They stared into each other's eyes with anxious, puzzled stares. Why was it necessary to leave each other? Why must she leave? Why was life so kind, then so cruel?

She held him fiercely tight for a moment, her fingers gripping his thin waist. "Oh, to leave you, to leave you—"

"Not to kiss you again. Not to touch you again. Not to see your body. Not to go into you and feel you shiver inside."

"Oh, Duane, I love you. I love you."

"My darling, I love you, I love you, love you."

They clung to each other, like children afraid of the dark.

"I don't want to leave you."

"I don't want you to go."

"Maybe we'll stay," said Susan.

"You mustn't," he said. "The kids shouldn't stay."

"I know. I know. But not to see you again—"

"Not to kiss you—"

He kissed her mouth, her throat, her breasts with the intensity of desperation.

"Do you love me?" she asked presently.

"I love you. You're the only one I've ever loved."

She could not say that. But she repeated the words he was hungry to hear. "I love you. You're my lover, my own love."

And holding him, she felt the hurt that must come to them at parting, the bewildered anguish when they could never embrace again.

CHAPTER SEVENTEEN

THE children had been coming home from school early this past week. Harvey said no more about "messing around with the gang." Coral seemed to have dropped Pam as a friend.

But Friday evening they did not come home on time. Susan ran to the front window every few minutes, but could not see them. Four o'clock, four-fifteen, four-thirty passed. Still they had not come.

She tried to reassure herself: the children had been kept after school. No, that wasn't likely. There might have been a class meeting. No, the children always told her if there would be anything like that.

All Susan could think of was the gang—and Coral Emmert. Coral was jealous and vindictive. She would not put anything past that girl.

By five, Susan was frantic. She put on her coat and hat and fairly ran the mile to the shopping center.

Duane was working in the back of the grocery. He looked up and saw her. "Susan! What's wrong?"

"The children—not home—worried. Have any of the gang—been around here?" She could not seem to get her breath.

He frowned. "No," he said sharply. "They usually hang around after school, but today I haven't seen any of them."

"What shall I do?" She felt cold with panic.

"I'm going to call the police."

He went over to the phone, dialed and talked briefly. Then he spoke to one of the other men, who nodded and handed him some keys.

He came back to Susan. "The police are coming. I've borrowed a car. Come on."

She followed him as he ran to the parking lot at the back of the store. "Where are we going?" she panted.

"The barn—the hideout of Goss's gang."

"Oh!"

She said no more in the brief ride past their house, out to the old tumbled-down barn in the muddy field. Duane turned the car into the lane and they bumped along the ruts up to the open barn doors. A red convertible was parked there, along with several jalopies.

"Fred Goss's car," said Duane. He jumped out and ran into the barn. Susan followed.

There was a crowd of boys in the barn, gathered around two shapes on the floor. The boys were laughing and yelling. She saw Coral Emmert leaning against a post, smoking a cigarette, her face somber and angry.

Susan saw one of the shapes on the floor.

"Harvey!" she screamed. The boy was lying sprawled out, his face cut and bleeding, his eyes closed. Susan shoved two boys out of her way to get to Harvey. They turned, startled.

"Hey—you—Hey, Fred! Here's their mom!"

Then Susan saw Pam. "Oh, my God!" she moaned.

The girl was lying naked on a pile of her own clothes.

Three boys held her down as she struggled feebly. Another boy was kneeling at her legs. They were laughing, their faces red with excitement.

Duane caught the boy about to rape Pam. He dragged him away, knocked him sprawling. Then he grabbed another boy. Susan got to Pam, and crouched over her.

"My Pam! Baby—Pam!"

She pulled off her coat, threw it over the girl. Pam's eyes were half-open, but dazed with shock. She did not seem to see her mother.

One of the boys tried to push Susan away. Susan clawed at him like a wildcat.

"You animals! Get away, you filthy little beasts!"

She saw Fred Goss near Carol. Susan cursed him furiously, but the boy only laughed. He flung his cigarette on the floor and came toward her. "Maybe you'd like some of what we were gonna give Pam."

The boys laughed, cheered him on. "Go on, Fred! Show her! Go on, get her!"

"Sirens!" screamed a boy. "Cops coming! Run!"

In a moment the boys were in a panic; they ran in all directions, like rats.

Susan held Pam, hugged her close. The girl was too quiet, too still.

The policeman came in the wide barn door, then another man entered.

"What is this? What—"

Susan looked up at the familiar voice. Paul, immaculate in his grey business suit, was staring down at them.

"Pam," he said incredulously. "Pam!"

The girl finally stirred. "Daddy," she muttered.

Paul knelt beside her. "Pam, sweetheart!"

Susan caught his hand as he moved the coat. She's naked," she told him. "They stripped hed."

Paul looked up at her. "Rape?" he whispered.

"Yes. I don't know if we—were in time."

"Oh, my God! Pam!"

"This your boy?" asked one of the policemen. He was carrying Harvey.

Paul staggered to his feet. "Yes. Yes! What happened?"

"He's out. Unconscious. Looks like he was beaten up. Couple head wounds look bad. We've sent for a doctor."

Paul looked around wildly. "What kind of a place is this?"

The policeman answered him. "This is an old barn where Goss had his hangout. We knew they had a sex ring, but we couldn't prove it till now."

"A—sex ring—"

"Yes. They get younger kids and bring them here. Have a regular circus. But the kids wouldn't talk. Well, we've got them this time."

Paul did not seem to know what to say or do. The policeman carried Harvey out to the ambulance they had sent for, then came back for Pam.

"You want to come with us?" the policeman asked Paul.

"Yes—oh, yes—" He seemed dazed.

"You'll have to drive the car, Paul. I'll go in the ambulance," Susan told him.

"All right." He seemed to be functioning in a daze.

When Harvey came to in the emergency ward, he told them a little of what had happened.

"After school, Pam and I started to walk home. Coral said—ride with Fred. Pam said no. Some boys grabbed me, put me in Fred's car. Said they'd beat me up unless she came too. I told her to run. But she came. They beat me up anyway. At the barn. Tried to stop them. Fought. Coral teasing Pam. Fred wanted to—rape her first. Argued about that. Coral said let other boys rape her first. Finally he said okay."

Paul groaned aloud. "Pam—little Pam," he said.

"I tried to stop them, Dad. I just couldn't fight them all."

"There were about twenty boys there. You did wonderfully, Harvey," Susan said.

"Guess I'll have to have some more fighting lessons," said Harvey, closing his eyes again.

"No, no more," said Paul, a white line around his mouth. "I've been a fool. A sex ring! My God! We're moving out of here as soon as I can find another place to live."

Susan would have rejoiced, but she was too concerned about Pam. The doctor finally finished his examination, and beckoned to Susan and Paul.

"She hasn't been raped."

"Thank God!" said Susan, shuddering with relief.

"She's in a state of shock, however." He advised them how to care for her.

"Can we take her home?"

"Yes. I think she'll be better off with you."

Harvey wanted to go home too, and the doctor released him. "But you stay quiet for a while, young man. And, please be careful of the head."

"Aw, I've got a tough head," said Harvey.

He limped out to the car, with Susan's arm around him. Paul carried Pam, dressed once more in her ripped school dress and coat. Susan carried the red tam, muddy and crushed.

For the first time she remembered Duane. She looked around for him. "Where did Duane go?"

"The boy from next door? He went down to police headquarters to testify. Say, that's quite a boy! He knocked out several of the kids, including the gang leader."

"He's been a good friend," said Susan soberly.

She put Pam to bed when they got home. The girl seemed able to move, but she could not speak. Susan was not sure she heard what they were saying. She clung tightly to Susan's hand as she bent over her in bed.

"Darling, do you want anything?"

"Mummy," whispered Pam.

"Can I get you anything?"

"Daddy."

Paul bent over her from the other side of the bed. "I'm here, darling. What can I do?"

"Mummy," she whispered.

That was all she could say. Susan stayed with her till she was asleep. Then she went downstairs to see how Harvey was getting along.

Paul had fixed supper, fumbling around the kitchen. Harvey was not hungry.

"My head feels as big as a balloon, and it hurts all over, down to my back," he complained.

"I think you'd better go to bed too," said Susan.

"I guess so." He stood up, wobbled a moment. "Whew! I'm dizzy." He started for the door.

Paul said, "I'll take you to your room." He put an arm around the boy. Susan heard him say in the hall, "I'm proud of you, fighting for your sister that way. You are a brave boy."

Susan sat down at the table, drank some coffee. The scene in the barn came back to her vividly. The laughing red-faced boys, the angry Coral, the nasty spoiled face of the older boy, Fred. What kind of monsters were they, to find pleasure in tormenting smaller children?

She covered her face with her hands. A few minutes more—a few minutes—and Pam would have been raped.

"Susan?" Paul's hand touched her lightly. She had not heard him come in. She raised her head.

"Yes, Paul."

He sat down beside her at the table. "Is that what you have been trying to tell me, all this time?"

She nodded. "I felt they were vicious, thrill-happy, spoiled, and dangerous."

"But if you'd only told me—a sex ring! My God!"

"I didn't know that. I guessed—but I never dreamed it was that bad." Her voice trembled.

"We'll move right back to Franklin," Paul decided abruptly. "They shall not go back to school here. It will be a few days anyway before they'll be strong enough to go to school. By that time we will be back in Franklin. All right, darling?"

She smiled at him, but in her weakness tears filled her eyes and started to slide down her cheeks. "All right," she choked.

He kissed her. "And you can have your social life again, your bridge club and concerts," he teased her.

"Just so Pam's all right. Just so she—oh, Paul, if her mind is affected—"

"Now don't borrow trouble. We'll have the doctor here every day. And we will move in a few days. That should help, getting away from here."

"Yes. It'll make a lot of difference. All the difference in the world." She wiped her eyes.

All the difference in the world ... Back to Franklin, the city she knew and loved. Away from Duane. Never to see him again, never to enjoy his embraces, to know his comforting, his understanding affection. All the difference in the world. She would get what she wanted—to return to Franklin. But there would be a loss also, a bewildering emptiness, when she could no longer know Duane.

CHAPTER EIGHTEEN

MONDAY evening Paul came home and announced abruptly he had put their house up for sale and had bought a new one in Franklin. Susan stared at him, wide-eyed. Harvey dropped his fork.

"Just like that!" gasped Harvey. "My gosh, Dad, can't we even see it first?"

"It's a good house, in an excellent neighborhood, in the school district you wanted, Susan," he said impatiently.

"I thought this time you'd tell us first, and let us help choose," said Harvey bluntly.

Paul turned a little red. "Since when do I need advice from my children on buying a house?"

"You didn't do so hot on this one!" said his son.

Susan hastened to smooth things over. "Where is the house, exactly, Paul? And how big is it?"

"It's as big as this one," he said. "I like a nice, big house." He explained the location. "Just three blocks from school."

"Gee, I'll be pals with Jim again!" Harvey was radiant. "We'll work on our experiments again. I bet he hasn't found anybody to help him since I left."

Susan was thinking with dismay about another large house. Her time would be so taken up with housework that she would have no time for photography. The job... She had not told Mr. Crandall whether she would take it or not.

"When are we going to move, Dad?" asked Harvey.

"As soon as Pam is able to," he said firmly. "I'll talk to the doctor tonight and see what he says."

The doctor thought they should go ahead and move, even if Pam had to move in an ambulance. "It'll do her a world of good to get away from here," he said.

Susan agreed. So Paul said he would see the movers on Tuesday and arrange a date. "Can you be ready by Thursday or Friday of this week?"

"Yes!" said Susan.

She did not care if all the dishes got broken in the morning, all the clothing mussed, the furniture damaged—just so they could get away.

She went to Pam's room and told her with quiet joy, "Daddy has bought a house in Franklin near your old school. And we're going to move as soon as we can get a moving van."

A flicker of interest came into Pam's half-closed eyes. "Franklin?" she murmured.

"Yes, darling. Back home. Won't that be good?" She watched the girl's face anxiously.

"Good," breathed Pam.

Pam seemed noticeably better the next day. Susan told her she was going to start packing immediately. Duane and Harvey were helping. Duane brought some cartons from the grocery store. Pam wanted to help too. Susan decided to let her get up and dress.

Pam sat on the couch, to watch while they worked.

Harvey said, "You can wrap dishes, Pam. I'll bring you a box and some papers."

Susan was about to protest. Duane shook his head at her.

"All—right," said Pam. She sat up and accepted the lapful of dishes Harvey carried to her. She was slow in wrapping each plate, but soon there was more color in her cheeks.

In the kitchen, Duane said, "Let her help. Harvey has the right idea. She needs to get her mind off what happened."

Harvey was cleaning the dining room dish cabinet with happy ruthlessness. They would have to eat off the kitchen plates until they unpacked in the new house. But who cared? Not Susan.

She decided to start lunch. At the rate the boys were working they would be starved. And maybe Pam would eat something besides toast and tea.

Duane was packing pans, fitting them neatly into the boxes.

"Duane, what are you going to do?" she asked abruptly. "You're not going to stay here, are you?"

"Not after you leave," he said.

"Where will you go?"

"I've been thinking. I've about decided to move to Columbus and try to get into State. I could work part-time, the way you said."

"Oh, that's good! I'm glad." She smiled at him, and he smiled back. "I'll miss you, so much. But I'm glad you'll be going to college. You'll make something of yourself."

"You're the one who's made something of me. Nobody cared about me before, so I didn't care either."

"I'm glad—you care now." She wanted to hug him, but she couldn't, with the children nearby.

"I thought I'd major in education—teach, like you said. Maybe in science. I always liked science."

"You'd be good in that."

"I'll get married some day, I suppose. But not for a long time."

"Why not?"

"It'll take a long time to forget you enough," he said.

"I'll never forget you," she said, softly. "You helped me when things were so dark, I couldn't see any hope at all."

Paul came home shortly before four o'clock. "The movers are coming Thursday. I thought I had better help pack."

She and Paul and Harvey packed for a time, then she fixed dinner. Pam had slept most of the afternoon. She seemed better, though she could not be as gay as Harvey was. It would be a long time, thought Susan, before Pam recovered from the shock.

That night, she and Paul went to bed late, bone tired. Paul had decided to take off the rest of the week from the office to help move. She lay in his arms. He had gone to sleep so rapidly that he had not made love to her. She felt too tired to sleep for a while.

She lay and watched the stars flickering in the black sky above New Harmony. They would leave in another two days. They would never have to come back here again.

In Franklin, they would go back to their old ways of life—of leisure, books, concerts, Harvey's scientific experiments, Pam's books and records and girl friends. Yet the summer and autumn here had made a mark on each of them that time would not be able to erase.

Harvey was tougher, more sure of himself. He could fight. He had learned to question adults, even his own adored father. He had learned to distrust, to hesitate, to withhold confidence. He would never be quite the trusting boy he had been.

Pam had grown up with shock. She too had learned to distrust, but she had not learned to fight. Susan worried about Pam. When she was older, would she fear men? What about dates— would she go willingly? And girl friends … She had trusted Coral to a certain extent. What would happen to Pam?

Paul was honestly sorry about what had happened. But he had changed least of all. He had bought the new house in Franklin as impulsively as he had this one, without consulting Susan or the children. He was still arrogantly sure that he knew best.

Susan came to a decision. For she of them all had changed the most in the harsh environment of New Harmony. Things were not going to be the same any more. She was not going to be blindly dependent on Paul.

She would learn to drive, and get a car of her own. Paul's dictum was absurd. She was not reckless and careless, as his aunt had been. There was no reason to think she would be a poor driver, just because she was a woman.

And she would take the job with *Field and City Street.* She lay wide-eyed, her heart thumping, as she realized her mind was really made up. It would make good use of her talents, it would give her independence and a chance to mature. And it would allow her to hire a housekeeper.

Paul would be angry, but he would get over it. He would not like it at first as she became more sure of herself, more competent, and self-confident. But he would get over that too.

She still loved Paul. They belonged together. But she was no longer blind to his faults. She would never again let herself and the children be so completely subject to his whims. He must learn to consult them before making decisions for all of them. Harvey would be more and more difficult to manage as he grew older, if Paul insisted on blind obedience.

Paul was only human, not divine, as Susan once thought him. She blamed herself for having let the situation become so serious before she did something about it. But it had taken her a long time to grow up. Growing up, maturing, was so painful that she had refused to face it until it had been forced on her.

Paul stirred sleepily, wakened. "Are you awake?" he muttered.

"Yes. I've been thinking."

His arms tightened around her. "You've changed this summer," he said. "You never made love with me before like that."

"Oh, I learned a lot," she said. "Quite a lot."

And some of the things he might not like, she thought, even as she turned to meet him. Her new convictions, her new independence, her strength in the face of his anger.

Then, as they became involved in a passionate embrace, she thought, "But life is going to be much more exciting this way!"

THE END